D1156728

The Southern Reporter

Other books by John William Corrington

SHORT STORIES
The Lonesome Traveller and Other Stories
The Actes and Monuments

NOVELS
And Wait for the Night
The Upper Hand
The Bombardier

POETRY
Where We Are
The Anatomy of Love
Mr. Clean and Other Poems
Lines to the South

The Southern Reporter

STORIES BY JOHN WILLIAM CORRINGTON

LOUISIANA STATE UNIVERSITY PRESS
BATON ROUGE AND LONDON 1981

DESIGNER: Patricia Douglas Crowder
TYPEFACE: Linotype Janson
TYPESETTER: Service Typesetting Co.
PRINTER: Thomson-Shore, Inc.
BINDER: John Dekker & Sons, Inc.

"Nothing Succeeds" was originally published in the *Southern Review*.

LIBRARY OF CONGRESS CATALOGING IN PUBLICATION DATA
Corrington, John William.
    The southern reporter
    CONTENTS: The man who slept with women. —Nothing
succeeds. —A day in thy court. —The great
pumpkin.—[etc.]
    I. Title.
PS3553.07S66   813'.54   80-26204
ISBN 0-8071-0869-3

A.M.D.G.
& for
Robert Edward Lee Corrington
&
Thomas Jonathan Jackson Corrington

—Confederates of mine

Contents

The Man Who Slept with Women

— You know how to handle women, my uncle Shad used to say down at the Glass Hat. — Shit on 'em. Don't ask 'em nothing, don't answer no questions, don't smile at 'em. If you talk, lie. If you buy 'em something, make sure you can hock it. Don't put no initials on anything. So you can give it to the next one when the one you got goes flat.

— Or starts swelling. Somebody would put in.

Uncle Shad should know. In a triangle formed by Kilgore, Texas, and Texarkana and Bossier City, Louisiana, Uncle Shad was known universally as a Mean Ass. With the exception of Bad Son of a Bitch, that was the most honorific title a man could hold. It signified that he was solitary, vicious, incapable of truth or charity, except within a limited circle of friends and kin, dedicated to every form of hedonism this side of sadism, not necessarily excepting certain forms of violence known only to a people who had passed from hogs and cotton, and whiskey-making to drilling, dusting, and bartending in less than a generation. Uncle Shad was my mother's brother, and he was celebrated wherever drinking, whoring, stomping, and wholesale outrage was the bill of fare. Which covered the greater part of Bossier City, especially Highway 80 toward Minden and Vicksburg east and Dallas west. Up and down that strip he stalked, strutted, slouched, and staggered. Drinking, kicking, biting, or swamping whatever rose (or fell) before him. And if there was one thing on God's misshapen earth he did dearly love, it was to drag me, his nephew, out of a night with him.

— Treat a whore like a lady . . . Uncle Shad would bawl.

— And a lady like a whore, all the roughnecks and tool pushers in the Tower Bar and Grille would yell back.

— And the world's rare snatch is gonna fall open for you like a sailor's satchel.

Because Uncle Shad despised my mother. He didn't hate her—no, he loved her. He truly did. But he despised her. He could not bear to touch her, and ten minutes was the outer limit of his ability to converse with her. She made him shudder.

Because she was very good. Good and most men thought beautiful, well married, thoroughly cultured and deeply religious.

— And she grew up in a cornfield five miles out of Tyler, Texas, without a pot to piss in or a window to throw it from. Daddy ran a pair of mules and later a tractor and worked up to croppin' shares whilst I learned the oil business and got sand in my ass from swallowing drilling mud. And your mother she went to work at the Woolworth's five and dime, and then at a restaurant called the Jumbo Grille and met your paw who was two years further on gargling mud than me. Who got lucky on account he had a head of naturally pure silver hair when he was nineteen, and the boss on that lease, Mr. Arch Riley, took twenty a week out of your paw's check for ole Whitey, and when he was twenty-one, called him down off a rig and handed him twenty-one thousand dollars in cash money and a sixty-fourth piece of forty-four thousand dollars a year. And said, get your funny-looking ass over to SMU and take a college degree in geology. And on the way, he picked up your

mother cause she had to have the reddest red hair he ever
seen, and said to her, we can make it, sugar. You get you a
degree in French literature, cause Jesus and Judas knows it
ain't a thing from here to Brownsville as cultured as a degree
in French literature. And in a couple of years, that's what
happened.

— How come I got brown hair, I asked Uncle Shad.

— Say, he said, eyes widening. — You sure do. Ain't that
the shits?

Uncle Shad weighed two hundred and forty except when
he went to fat. Then it was two-eighty, but you couldn't
tell. He was six foot three and very meaty around the face
with chops for jaws and a wide, heavy-lipped mouth that
looked all right because of his size. And small brown almost
kindly intelligent eyes that were pressed far back on either
side of a nose so often broken that you only speculate on
what it had originally looked like.

When he smiled, there was no guile in it, and people
wanted to love him. My father loved him. Possibly more
than he loved mother. He would have spent most of his time
drinking with Uncle Shad except he was usually in Beirut
or Lisbon, Cairo or Kuwait, and Uncle Shad would not
leave the Texas-Louisiana border for any amount of money
my father had yet thought to offer. The last figure Shad
had turned down was thirty thousand a year as honcho in
what he called one of those chickenshit heathen kingdoms
down in the Persian Gulf's steaming crotch.

— Maybe it was the French literature, Uncle Shad said at
last, cracking another can of Schlitz.

— Huh?

— Huh what, you skinny little bastard?

— I mean, sir.

— You bet your scrawny ass you mean, sir. Maybe the
French literature made you have brown hair.

I didn't see that. — How, Uncle Shad?

— How do I know? It sure turned your momma inside out. Last time I come to the house, she says *entre nous*, Shadrach ... *vis-à vis* Tommy ... Listen, she wanted to talk about your milieu and your something or other. Said I was bad for all of em.

— What did daddy say?

— Didn't say shit. He was in Mexico City. You know, if I'd been born with a head full of silver hair, they'd of reamed out a mare's ass with me and then claimed I was too old for the workmen's compensation act. Your poppa ...

We drove down to Blue's Red Devil. We always kept moving because after Uncle Shad picked me up at Byrd High School and I didn't show for dinner, Momma would start phoning. By now she would have got hold of the Bossier Parish sheriff and started some song and dance about them letting a fifteen-year-old minor do the joints in company of a dangerous madman, blood kin and local custom aside. And seeing the kind of money my father's company spread in Bossier Parish, they would come looking. But they knew the whole story, and they would start at the nearest bar to the Red River, the Hurricane, and work out. By the time they hit the Ming Tree, we would be at the Wooden Shoe. By the time they had a drink and try at the Shoe, we would have bypassed the Skyway Club which had fallen to ruin anyhow with Earl Blessey's band cut out and would be at the Tower Bar and Grille. They always came across us at the Mistletoe, a deadly wretched place with barmaids who were too far gone in age, vice, or disease even for the Tower.

— Thanks to Jesus for canned beer, Uncle Shad would mutter, studying the girl who brought five cans through the gloom and a Seven-Up for me.

Then Deputy Pritchard would arrive. He was short, bald, mild-eyed, and faintly ridiculous in his Stetson and boots, with one khaki pants leg in and one out. There was no way on earth to see Deputy Pritchard as dangerous. Which was odd, considering he had killed six or eight men over the years in single combat, and had won the National Pistol Championship in 1948.

— Pritch, Uncle Shad would say, — you can have this here beer or kiss my ass.

Deputy Pritchard would shake his head and lift his belly as he slid into the booth beside me. — It ain't no choice, he would answer. — Why don't you hand me that beer.

And they would talk. It was a ritual and almost without variance. Uncle Shad would ask questions, and Deputy Pritchard would answer. Then Deputy Pritchard would ask and my uncle answer. There was virtually no exchange of information at all. Which was just fine because they were not talking to exchange information, but to touch one another with words, reassure each other of continuing amity and respect. They had grown up on the rigs together, and one had saved the other's life or something, which I never was able to make out and had no chance to ask about and the straight of which even they may not have recalled. Then when the beers and the doings were satisfactorily done, Deputy Pritchard would turn to me as if he had only then noticed that I occupied the corner of his booth.

— Son, he would say gravely, — your momma give us a call. She seemed to think you had gone off with some crazy man.

— His momma can fuck a bull baboon, Uncle Shad would mutter.

Deputy Pritchard was always amazed. — I'll overlook that kind of talk, seeing it's your own blood kin. But I never heard such talk about a lady ...

— You'll overlook it cause I'll pull off your arm and stuff it up your dying ass, Uncle Shad would grin dangerously.

Deputy Pritchard would purse his lips and shake his head.
— I believe your momma was right, boy. This here man is
a dangerous lunatic.

— No, I would answer, making one of my first entries
into the rough stylized banter of men, — he's my uncle.

— You mean, Deputy Pritchard's eye widened, — This
here is the widely known bad man Shadrach Courtney?

— The same, Uncle Shad would say, smiling.

— The one without no balls, no brains, no guts? The one
they call the living miracle?

Then Uncle Shad would reach under the table and dig
his fingers into Deputy Pritchard's thigh just above the knee
or reach across and put a neck lock on him. People sitting
at the tables or dancing to the jukebox would pause and
move aside, not knowing for sure whether it was funning or
serious. Knowing only that both or either of them there in
the booth with a skinny fifteen-year-old could clean out the
place single-handed, and that anything serious between them
was likely to work harm for a wide circle all around.

Then they would break it off and grin at one another,
finish the last of their last beers, and we would leave.

It would be late by then, and cool, and we would stand
outside in the gravel of the parking lot and they would swap
stories of sexual heroism or reports of new degeneracy.
They would talk about women they had both known and
the legends of endurance and cruelty from those days.
Shootings and cuttings, accidents and assassinations. Deputy
Pritchard would chronicle the newest wave of whores re-
puted to be working the town, and oftener than not, Uncle
Shad would evaluate them one by one and list them according to his own arcane system.

— It ain't no use with the blond at Kim's. I bought her
three drinks. But she's waiting for love.

— Reckon if you told her you had ten thousand
dollars . . . ?

— That's love.

— Maybe you could send her to college, Deputy Pritchard began.

— Lay off that shit, Uncle Shad answered. — College could of ruined the pussy of the Queen of Sheba.

— That boy goin' to college?

— I'd as soon put him out on the grass.

Then we would climb into Uncle Shad's jeep and wave to Deputy Pritchard and head back toward Caddo Parish and my mother's cold, inarticulate, exceptionally well-bred anger.

All my life I had heard about hard rows to hoe. By the time I came along—which is to say by the time Mother decided to have me—the rows and the hoes were pretty much all gone. We had three gardeners and a tree surgeon from Lambert's nursery on retainer. But there are other rows and other hoes. Me? I had Mother. Who, once she decided to have me, having me, decided to have me all the way. I was sixteen the summer in question, and, sure as God lost a boy, I was still sleeping with Mother. Whenever my father was out of town. Which was mostly. I didn't like it. It gave me the creeps. But what are you going to do? I kind of wanted to tell my father, but there never seemed to be time, and anyhow, I could hear the conversation as it might well go, and it seemed creepier than the fact. So I told Uncle Shad.

— My God, it's unnatural. Does she . . . Lord, I knew she'd gone all to hell, but that French stuff.

It seems he'd mentioned my mother's college major to one of his pub-crawling pals, who in turn introduced him to de Sade and Restif de la Bretonne. — Lord, he said again, rubbing his chops. — We got to do something about this. We got to . . .

He didn't enlarge on the something. But instead of us just crossing paths at the Glenwood Drug Store every once in a while, Uncle Shad started picking me up after school before Cromwell, Momma's Jamaican chauffeur, showed up. Then we'd eat and maybe catch an early movie, go by the tame joints in downtown Shreveport, and fall in on Bossier City like a ton of fists and pimples. And, after a month or two of this, I was beginning to catch on. I saw a lot, and I never was stupid. By the time we started for home each time, things were getting clearer and clearer. Home was just a place, not a permanent illness.

II

Only this particular night we never made it. Just below the new bridge we were doing maybe fifty-five, splitting the difference between Bossier City's speed limit of 35 and Uncle Shad's normal cruising speed of 75. Uncle Shad was drinking out of a bottle he kept in a brown paper sack under the front seat. Between sips, he was talking to me.

— Next time out, we'll go down to Mississippi. I got a friend runs a blind tiger and has him two hundred acres. When the revenuers get close, he goes to shooting deer out of season, and when the game wardens get the wind, he fires up that still again. Something going on year around. Two years ago, one of them revenue men shot the kneecap off a game warden. While Eddy and some friends laid out in the brush watching, drinking popskull and eating venison.

Just then, out of the corner of my eye, I saw a blur pull out of a side street as fast as a doe downwind. Then nothing. I didn't feel or hear anything. It was like being a television set and somebody got tired, yawned, and turned me off. I hope to Christ dying is like that.

Next thing I knew, I came back on, and it felt like I was in the middle of some crazy commercial. I couldn't make out where I was, and colors and shapes ran into one another something fierce. I could hear Uncle Shad. He was talking close by. Not loud, but very earnest.

— I tell you what. If this little old boy dies, I'm gonna start off making you fuck a furnace . . .

There was water all over the place. Maybe we had hit a space-warp like in *Amazing Wonder Tales* and I had got thrown into a fountain in the Place de la Concorde. Anyhow, it was coming down all over me, and I was spread-eagled out on my belly. But I couldn't feel my legs much, and I seemed to be jackknifed around the middle somewhere. Breathing was a bad go. I realized I was grabbing one mouthful of air at a time like a fish on the bank. It scared me a little, but I was still half off, and it seemed I had been breathing that way for a long time.

— And then I'm gonna make his momma a necklace out of your roasted nuts . . .

There were red lights flashing, and white and black things moving around, and way off I could hear what sounded like the whole Shreveport police department coming on with their sirens high. Somebody started lifting me up.

— On the other hand, if he's all right, I'm just gonna give him a baseball bat and a bad bulldog and let him see to you himself.

Then Uncle Shad was leaning over me. — Looks like somebody run you through a screen door. How does it feel?

— What feel? I got out.

— Your face, you dumb bastard.

— Face?

He shrugged and let whoever it was unwind me from whatever it was I had gotten wrapped around. But he looked worried, and that pleased me. Maybe my mother's blood was inside after all. If it was, a good deal was leaking out. Anyhow, as they pulled me up, I could see that the top half of me had gone through the jeep's windshield. They had sprayed it and the old wreck we'd hit to keep off fire before they untangled me. Then I could see the little colored man Uncle Shad still had by his collar, talking to him in that even, conversational tone. He looked like I felt, and drunk to boot. A couple of Bossier City police were standing beside them, trying halfheartedly to pry Uncle Shad's fingers out of the little fellow's shirt. They lowered me to the stretcher about then, and I felt like I was dropping to the bottom of a very expensive dry hole. Which is when that same cosmic viewer got bored once more, and I got turned off again.

III

For my next exploit, they had rigged me out in a white robe that covered my front and tied in back, leaving me bare-assed as a heifer at a hayride. And everything but my eyes was bandaged from my neck to the top of my head. I felt like some king's twin brother or a package left over from Christmas. There were people fooling around on the other side of the room, and of course one of those jugs full of water up over the bed with a length of rubber hose running down to my arm. And folding up sheets just at the edge of my vision, a blond who had almost made redhead with a twat that would pull up the blood pressure on a mummy. I felt awful, but that girl whose face I hadn't even seen, had me ready to eat. I wouldn't have minded dinner, either.

Then came the deluge. I could hear her all the way down the corridor outside:

— Don't lie to me. He's dead.

— No, somebody said, not sounding especially happy about it.

— He's crippled for life. Say it. I can take it. Don't lie to me. I can't stand a son of a bitch lies to women.

— No, actually . . .

— Actually, when you went in for exploratory, you found out his spine . . .

— No . . .

— Something worse? His little genitals . . . ?

I reached down before he could answer, and whispered
along with him:

— No . . .

— My son, my only son is in there, and you won't tell
me . . . what . . . if you have pity for a mother's . . .

— He has contusions, multiple lacerations, and possible
internal . . .

— Internal. *Injuries.* She said, sounding like a pathologist
on *Young Doctor Malone.*

— Possible.

All this time, I wasn't just dead positive it was her. At
first her voice was high and harsh, something stringy and
mean in it. Then, when she got to asking about my little
parts, it dropped back to that fine Pierremont contralto I
was used to. It was Mother, all right.

— Possible, she repeated, her voice moving into the upper
reaches of baritone. — Will he . . .

— Ma'am?

— Will he . . . be all right?

— Oh, yes ma'am . . .

— You're lying like a dog, she told him smoothly.

— I can see it in your eyes. Shad's run him into a wall and
made a vegetable out of him, right?

— Oh no . . .

— How much is that drunken son of a bitch paying you?
Don't you know I can tell? Don't you know you can't
hide it from a mother? Don't you know I'll sue the ass off
this place for false pretenses, pain and suffering, misrep-
resentation . . .

— Ma'am, would you like to go in?

She came through the door with this tall young doctor
who looked like he could use some of my jug himself. She
was dressed like it was show time at the Stork Supper Club,
complete with that damn silly-looking silver fox thing and

platinum earrings I had tried to steal once or twice. — He's probably got no more mind left than a horsefly. Sonny, she said, staring down into my bandages. — Sonny darling, speak to me. Speak to your mother.

— Glaaah, I said. — Gro-gro-gro. Whaag.

The doctor slumped against the wall, and for the smallest split second mother's eyes opened wide. Then she started to swing at me and caught herself. — Thank God, she sighed, her fingertips touching the snood of gauze that kept me from biting them. — Your mind's not gone.

She pulled up a chair and sat down beside the bed while the doctor, scarce recovered, busied himself around my bed. When he reached to take my pulse, I pulled my wrist loose and went to scratching my crotch. Like the Red Cross nurse on the poster, he wanted to serve. But what kind of guy tries to get to a good-looking woman through her injured child?

— All he's done is destroy your face. Nothing much, mother went on, her voice now controlled and cosmopolitan again, that touch of unidentifiable accent, that sweet gut-tuned contralto moving like syrup in the room's small echoless extent. As she ended each sentence, that eternal note of sadness managed to creep in. It almost broke, that succulent voice: madonna, Livia, Medea. Something like a song, like a sob.

— He's evened the score. By turning my baby into a monster.

— Grr, I said. Even without bandages, on my feet and moving, I used gutterals, monosyllables, grunts, and certain vague shiftings of the shoulders when it was necessary to converse with Mother. What the hell, was Jesus a big talker when mom was on the scene? Does the ice cube know what puts the cold on it? Then the Young Malone gave up. Short of an enema or something strange, there was nothing

else he could even fake doing for me. I guess he thought of
it and passed on the enema. The other he had in mind for
Mom. If only he knew.

— You worthless reproduction of your old man, she
whispered to me as the door closed behind the white knight.
— You creepy little bastard. No, don't gargle at me. One
lousy croak or cough and I'll pour this pitcher of water in
your mouth and nose holes.

She'd do it. She really would. She was like an artist whose
canvas won't hold still when it came to me. She had this
vision of a handsome prep-school, football and maybe even
polo player wearing a crimson blazer and doing the Rhodes-
scholar bit and all. What she gets is atavism. Back to the
khakis and axle grease. 30.06 Springfields in the fall and a
growing determination to squirm into the very bowels of
Caddo and Bossier Parish lowlife. With Uncle Shad playing
Virgil in a jeep. This is rough on a little old East Texas
girl who parlayed sweet legs, a wild backside, generous
superstructure and a random grab at a silver-haired Energy
Source into maybe 10 or 12 million dollars with trimmings.
The trouble with big money is, you feel obligated to do
something with it. When you run through cars, pools,
houses, clothes and maybe a couple of jaunts while the
Energy Source is out supplying the world, you cast about.
And discover you've got a kid. Ahah. *Now what do you
reckon he might do, become, think, be, if I was to.* Off to
the races. Except Shad is all over the dark hours with a
passkey to the underground. Oho. And those late-night
occasional phone calls I've been getting long-distance from
my father for almost a year. Coming with scary regularity
just when I need them. As if Uncle Shad is keeping him
plugged in. A hundred and fifty dollars will get you 10 or
15 minutes on Southern Bell from almost anywhere to might
near everyplace.

— I'd just as soon leave it go, I said finally, one hand in my crotch and the other hovering under the sheet to guard my mouth and nose holes.

She slapped the arms of the chair. — Well I ain't. Not near. She was getting mad again and that far-off wild-assed Davy Crockett twang was coming on, along with some home-style grammar. Right there, between the cultivated and the vicious, you could love her. If you had a soul made for loving and fast as a blacksnake.

— I'm gonna camp here till I can get a look at what that godforsaken drunkard has left me.

— You? How come you? It's my crummy face.

— Your face your ass. Who do you reckon will have to pay for the surgery to get rid of the scars?

Ahah. I hadn't thought of that. Maybe one long livid white scar down the side of my jaw like the son of a bitching Desert Fox or something. Then I thought: with my luck, fate has randomly distributed across my face a grid of nine squares filled with smaller scars in the shape of noughts and crosses.

— What do you bet daddy pays for it, I snickered.

— For all your father knows, she answered, getting control again, — I buried you a week and a half ago out at Forest Park Cemetery. I tried to get hold of him all evening. Nobody in Paris or Rome knows where he is. Somebody said, try Indonesia. Which is not a city, but some heathen backwoods country full of reds and Chinamen.

— The Chinamen are reds, I told her, not sure of that, but wanting a cheap point.

— Never mind. Your father is out of it.

Oho. True. Has been out of it for a long time. Meets me once in a while coming in as I'm going out to school. Or vice versa. Once we played tennis and he strained his back letting me win and trying to make it look straight. He is the living image of the Man from Glad. So help me God, the first time I saw that commercial, I thought I'd faint. Then I saw it was Union Carbide, which he doesn't own yet, and laughed through a pair of cheese sandwiches and a beer somebody left in the upstairs refrigerator. Oh dad, poor dad. Hell, poor me. I didn't not love him. I loved him like a picture of Roy and Trigger I got when I was four. But you get so tired of throwing out all those rays of gee and wow, and getting back a big emptiness. Sooner or later the signals weaken, and love is something you remember and approve. But it's in the inactive file. Man from Glad, how would you like a boy about sixteen who doesn't know his ass from Buck Rogers and is badly mauled about the head and ears? That's what I thought.

— Listen, I'm going to get the nurse to stay with you, my mother said. — While I go find out if you can go home. You'd rest better at home.

— No, I said, listen . . .

But she didn't listen, and I was talking to the door. For a minute. Then it opened, and that blond groin-grabber came into the room. At flank speed. I thought maybe they had me wired, and the board lights were saying I had gone critical on them. But then, right behind her came Uncle Shad, one hand about four inches away from her twat. The four-inch gap was explained by the fact that his other arm was filled with boxes.

— Honey, you move like you was mounted on twenty-one jewels, Uncle Shad whispered hoarsely. — Now you just stay put there for a little bit.

Then he turned to me. — Boy, you asleep?

— Mother's here.

— So you ain't asleep. Or likely to be. Listen, I brung you some stuff.

One of the boxes was Chicken Delight. Ten assorted backs and wings. I think I like backs and wings best. Mother swore it was because my father and Uncle Shad ate nothing else. More likely it was because she always made me eat the breast when I was little. Uncle Shad said he didn't even know a chicken had a breast till he was twenty, away from home and buying his own. — Which was six years after I found out girls had 'em. Ain't that odd?

Another box was full of Budweiser. — If you're old enough to get broke up, you're old enough to get boozed up, he said, placing the last box, the biggest one, on my sheeted legs. The box was leaking a yellow liquid. — Pickles and stuff, I asked.

— No, he said, pulling it open and lifting out some wriggling something. — It's a bulldog puppy.

— Mr. Shad, the nurse said, — I don't think . . .

— Sugar, do I know you? Uncle Shad turned and moved toward her. — I just feel I know you.

She was a good nurse and a hard case. Didn't stir an inch. Stood her ground smiling. — No sir, you don't. But you knew my momma. She . . .

— Your momma. Why sure, Uncle Shad said, getting an arm around her shoulders in friendly fashion as he dropped the puppy back on my legs, — And your momma used to work . . .

— At Schumpert Hospital, the nurse said, still not backing and filling like a sensible girl.

— She wasn't no nun, was she? he asked, letting his arm drop around her waist.

— Oh Mr. Shad, no. She did the night emergency desk and one night . . .

— My God, when Larry Milby tore loose my ear, and there was this angel right straight out of heaven . . .

— Yessir, and she . . .

— She sure did, and we . . .

— Yessir, youall did, and she never apologized nor anything, my momma didn't, and anyhow she . . .

Meanwhile the puppy and I were staring at each other.

He was either in shock or bilious, because he didn't pay the Chicken Delight any mind. He was pug-faced and irritable looking, and seemed mature for his size. But I could feel him trembling against my legs.

— Would you like a little Chicken Delight, Uncle Shad asked the nurse. — Or a Bud? Your momma was partial to rye whiskey. Drunk nearly a quart sitting up with me to see that ear didn't fall off and get swept away.

— Yessir, no, I mean I don't want any chicken and I can't have a Bud on duty, but momma . . .

Uncle Shad was kissing her neck and backing her over toward the bathroom door. She was holding her own, but not doing much to settle him down. Caught in the flush of maidenhood by a legend, I thought, as the puppy stalked up my legs and sniffed his way onto my chest. Her mother ought to have kept her mouth shut. Also I was hoping that bulldog puppy had pretty much done his duty before Uncle Shad unboxed him. Just then the phone beside my bed rang, and the blond nurse tried to go for it. But Uncle Shad had her pretty well, as you would say, in hand.

— Honey, what do they call you? Uncle Shad asked, getting her just inside the bathroom door and his hand just inside her uniform. Where the RN badge was pinned.
— Catch that goddamned phone, he called back over his shoulder as the door closed.

— They call me Teenie, the nurse was telling him.
— I sure don't know why, Uncle Shad cooed, and that was the last I heard. For a while.

With all those bandages, the phone was beyond my line of sight, so I had to fumble for it. As I finally got hold of it, mother came booming back through the door.

— Hello, I said into the phone, pressing it against the gauze over my ears.
— Hello yourself, mother answered. Then she stopped cold, staring at the Chicken Delight and the beer. The

puppy had lost his control and was throwing up down at
the foot of the bed. I didn't blame him.

— Hello?

— Mr. Thomas Thompson, plu-eeze, some mechanical
operator petitioned.

— You got him.

— Go ahead, plu-eeze.

— Hello?

And from a distance so vast that the call must have been
placed light-years ago, I could hear him. The voice was
tiny and twiny, but it was his, and I could see him in a white
suit, his face tanned and carefully honed by providence for
Great and Remembered poker games.

— ... Remember Princip ... ?

— Sir? ...

— ... in Serajevo ... Herzegovina. Remember your his-
tory? They ... Ferdinand ...

— Sure, yessir, I remember.

— ... Said you got banged up. You all right? ...

— Yessir, I'm fine, just a couple of cuts and ...

— ... Coming home soon as ... You never saw such ...
mountains. Like Spain or Tennessee ... want?

— Nothing. I'm just fine.

— Who *is* that, my mother wanted to know. Is that ... ?

— Tell Shad it's all fine. Salvation everywhere ... Tell
him to hold Caddo and Bossier and East Texas together.

— Yessir. What should I tell ... mother?

— What? she asked, reaching for the phone. — Let me
talk.

— Nothing, I heard from that enormous distance. — I'll be
home ... just get some rest ... you hear?

— Yessir, and then she wrenched the phone from my hand
and clapped it to her ear. — Tommy, she started. — Tommy?
Then she put the phone down on the bed, a peculiar ex-

pression on her face. Like when she had first seen the bulldog puppy: mingled distaste and disbelief, each struggling
to oust the other.

— It's a dial tone. There's nobody on that phone. I believe
you *have* lost your reason.

— Oho, I told her. — It's a magic phone. There's never
anybody on it unless you believe there is. If you don't believe, all you get is the dial tone.

— Anyway, she said, pursing her lips, ignoring my lunacy,
— Anyway, how could he find out less than two hours . . .
where the hell did that . . . The bull puppy had taken his
life in his paws and jumped to the floor. He was lurching
about, trying to find something.

— And this beer . . . Jesus Christ, all you need is a six-piece
band and some floozies . . .

She stopped dead, a can of beer in her hand. You never
saw such a look. Orphan Annie eyes. Mouth like a tragic
mask. —Oh, that wretched son of a bitch. Where is he? You
tell him to take that goddamn beer and that goddamn puk-
ing bulldog, and . . . if he shows up again in this . . .

Just then the bulldog puppy sniffed what he was after
and lumbered into the bathroom door. It opened easily, and
there was blondie, her dress down and up, too, and Uncle
Shad with something down and something up.

— Mon dieu, mother gasped, and I was proud of her. It
showed real self-breeding. Meanwhile the bulldog pup was
up on his hind legs lapping water out of the commode, and
Uncle Shad was trying to lever the door closed again with
his elbow or his foot or anything he had free to operate
with. But I was proud of him, too. He never even considered calling it a night. Finally, mother went over and pushed
the door to. Then she came back and sat beside the bed,
stunned.

— They said you could go home in the morning.

— No, I said. — I need rest.

— At home . . .

— . . . is where I can't rest. Maybe a glorious month in Herzegovina . . .

— Where?

— . . . or Bossier. I don't know.

— Tom . . .

She never had called me anything but honey or baby. Tom sounded all right.

— We could take a trip . . .

— No, I said. — Maybe next time.

She was angry and puzzled, but that fine feeling for how things were, that power of atmosphere analysis that had carried her from cotton patch to crystal palace never missed a vibration. She knew just how it was. And what to do.

— Well, she said. — You tell Shad I'm surprised at him.

— Sure, I said. — Sure you are. I'll tell him.

She still had a beer in her hand. — You mind if I take this?

— Drink it in good health, I told her.

— Your daddy says that.

— I know.

She was at the door. Not wanting to leave. Dead certain she'd better. — Was that . . . phone call . . . ?

— Why Momma, I said, — it was the Bossier Brothel, Incorporated. Wanting to know how that nurse was working out.

The door shut quietly, and I eased back. Sometime they had given me a shot or a pill so I'd sleep. So I thought I'd cooperate. Just as I was taking off for Bosnia, or Bossier, I heard Uncle Shad's voice. He was talking to the nurse.

— You got to be kiddin'. And she's sixteen? looks like your twin sister? Wants to be a nurse? Lissen sweetheart, you tell your momma me and my nephew are gonna come by and . . .

Then he was over my bed, looking at me, the nurse under one arm and that sullen bull pup under the other. — Lissen, I got news for you, he was saying.

As best I could, I turned back on for a minute,— And I got some news for you, I said.

Nothing Succeeds

I

Mr. Landry came to himself sitting on the terrace of the Forum, a Turkish restaurant. On Telegraph Avenue. In Berkeley, California.

In front of him, past a plate of lamb pilaf and a glass of retsina, out beyond the ornamental metal fence which divided the premises from the street, a young man without shirt, shoes or socks was on his knees in front of a young woman who appeared to be wearing only a poncho. The young man's hands were under the lower draping of the poncho, and he was caressing the young woman in a manner not to be described. And this in the soft chill twilight, just before dusk, in that city across from the city by the bay.

— My God, young Fourier gasped. — This place . . . Sodom by the sea . . .

Mr. Landry said nothing. He had already committed his indiscretion for this trip. Flying from New Orleans, he had had three martinis, three glasses of wine, and three Courvoisiers. His head hurt and his sentiments were vague. He could not quite believe in the reality of what was passing before him. He remembered now why men drank. To spare themselves reality. Considering what lay out there, he could not blame them. He had not drunk so much since those days in the Kappa Sigma house. At Tulane. In 1926, in the fall.

— I see it, but I don't believe it, young Fourier was saying. — It's like a show. Like some crazy son of a bitch putting all his dreams on a stage, one after another.

Young Fourier half rose to his feet. He had found another tableau now. A street band of incredibly dirty and hairy men, some young, some not so young, standing on the sidewalk half a block down, playing, singing. They would whip their guitars and pass from hand to hand a single cigarette. The music was not unpleasant. The words were unclear and distant. Something about John's Band. At one point, the guitar accompaniment fell away, and Mr. Landry was almost shocked by the wonderful purity of the few bars of *a capella* that followed. He shook his head. The young man and the young woman still stood in front of the Forum, still engaged in their rite. The only difference was that now the young woman had begun to move sinuously in time to the distant music. The young man began to nibble the young woman's thigh.

—Maybe he's broke, young Fourier snickered. — Maybe he can't afford anything . . . to eat. Young Fourier coughed, appalled at his own words. He had had six martinis, nine glasses of wine, and Courvoisiers beyond his counting on the way out from New Orleans. The curse and the temptation of first-class air travel. He was LSU School of Law, 1963, well aware that Mr. Landry suspected him of bestial tendencies. Tulane peopled the law offices of New Orleans, as a rule. The country parishes were left to LSU. It was supposed that Tulane produced gentlemen. Still, young Fourier had been at the top of his class. Mr. Landry had taken a chance. Now young Fourier glanced at Mr. Landry, who was squinting down at the band.

— I think it's the Grateful Dead, young Fourier volunteered.

— God rest their souls, Mr. Landry said, and sipped his retsina.

They had come to California to find Lancelot St. Croix
Boudreaux III. He had been gone some five years now,
gone, as the Civil Code had it, from his domicile, his ordinary place of habitation. No one in Breauxville had heard
from him. No one on the Island had the slightest idea where
he might be. The last word from him had been a large
dog-eared postcard mailed from Sausalito. It had had a picture of Sather Gate on the front, and on the other side, a
line of barely intelligible scrawl in Greek. The Old Man
had sent for Mr. Landry, who had translated it for him. Mr.
Landry well remembered Colonel Lance Boudreaux, body
twisted with age and arthritis, sitting propped in an ancient
rattan chair on the sun porch of the Mansion.

— Well, the Old Man had asked, — what the hell does
it say?

— It says, "Rejoice with me, for I have conquered the
Kosmos."

The Old Man had stared at him malevolently. — René, I
don't need a goddamned joke. What's that supposed to
mean?

Mr. Landry had shaken his head. — It . . . I don't know.
Christ said it . . . somewhere.

— If I could get hold of that crazy young son of a
bitch . . .

But he couldn't. Mr. Landry knew how much money the
Old Man had spent trying. Detectives. Special investigators.
A Louisiana state trooper placed on detached service as a
favor to the man who dominated agriculture in South
Louisiana. One report had come back from the trooper and
then silence. It was generally thought that he had defected
and might be found somewhere in San Francisco with a
flower between his teeth, mind and body rotted by dangerous drugs and controlled substances, more easily obtained
there than good licorice down home. Anyhow, no one in
Breauxville or on the Island had any idea what Sather Gate

was, and no one, including Mr. Landry, who had at least the advantage of having lived in New Orleans since his college days, could say what Lance might mean about conquering the Kosmos. That year, the rice and hot-pepper farmers on the Island and around the town were worried about the weather. There had been a novena for rain at the Immaculate Conception Church. The rain had come, and there was a big thanksgiving festival. Colonel Boudreaux, volatile as the pepper sauce which had made his family fortune almost a century before, had built and dedicated an altar to Mary Queen of Heaven. Even he had no illusions about how to deal with the Kosmos.

Mr. Landry shivered. It had turned chilly now, and the lights along Telegraph Avenue had come on. The parade of the peculiar had not ceased. The band was playing something about a dire wolf, and youths in leather jackets and Kit Carson rawhides, girls with indian feathers and Betty Boop makeup stood about listening, smoking. One boy with a Mohawk haircut, wearing only a loincloth, was stretched out on the sidewalk insensible. He had not moved for quite a spell. But no one paid him any mind, and Mr. Landry supposed people knew whether he was all right or not. He drank more wine, and thought that he should have brought winter clothes. It was summer here, and almost as cold as a New Orleans winter day. Hate California, it's cold and it's damp, Mr. Landry thought randomly. My God, that warning from so long ago. Tommy Dorsey and His Clambake Seven. It was not the weather of Louisiana. Nothing about California was like Louisiana.

— . . . the list, young Fourier was saying. — We go up to the university tomorrow. A professor in eastern religion. Some physicist . . . the police . . .

They had come to find Lance Boudreaux, to take him home. At least to tell him that he was universal legatee to his grandfather's estate, that he was heir not only to the

Island and to 6000 acres of prime farm land on the mainland growing peppers and rice and cane, but to the factory and the business itself, which turned a yearly profit of millions sending the Island's torrid pepper sauce to countries everywhere, most of which had not even existed in 1869 when the first Boudreaux had managed to scrape together enough money to purchase the Island from a carpetbagger who had been shot up on four separate occasions, whose cabin had been burned down with fearsome regularity every time he had left it to go into Breauxville to purchase supplies. All together, the estate was estimated to be worth some seventeen million for tax purposes. In fact, thirty-five million was more like it.

Eight days before, L. St. Croix Boudreaux I had died on the Island. Mr. Landry had been there. As he had been present at every important event in the chronicles of the Boudreaux family since 1927, when he had taken over from his father a law practice begun in 1880 when the first Breauxville Landry had come home from Rome, Georgia, after fifteen years of wandering beyond that day when he had been cast loose from Forrest's cavalry after his nation died. Mr. Landry had continued to take care of the Boudreaux business even after he had moved to New Orleans and established a staid and careful banking and real estate practice there. He kept a home near the Gulf and a tiny office in Breauxville chiefly for the Old Man, who would trust no one but him. Not because the Colonel had any great opinion of his legal talents, but because the Old Man never changed anything. He could abide sin, but the very idea of change seemed demonic to him, hence Mr. Landry, who was perhaps less rigorous on the point, but felt guilty because of his willingness to meet the times as they came, had never even attempted to suggest that another lawyer, closer to home, would be more immediately available to the Island and its master's needs. And the years had gone by. Mr.

Landry could remember when he was a boy fresh out of
law school, and the Old Man was no more than forty. He
had seemed immortal, as if the Island would sink and the
land turn to granite before he would be stirred, moved to
leave this place where his people had been so long. But, Mr.
Landry thought, looking out and up at the cold dark green
shadows of alien hills, nothing endures. Things change.
There is a succession of all things. We rise into light, stare
into the sun, and then pay the penalty to time for our
existence. Nothing succeeds but succession, he thought
wryly. What was that phrase they always used in law
school? *Le mort saisit le vif.* The dead enseize the living.
The living have nothing not willed them by the dead.
Not even life itself.

The Old Man had died hard. It had been a lonely death
in the Mansion there on the Island. Covered with ginger-
bread, the legacy of the first Boudreaux who had come to
the Island a hero for no other reason than taking it from
some yankee scum hated for his Anglo name by whites and
blacks alike, the house had grown as each new generation
had come along, until in the time of the old man, the family
had begun to shrink. Colonel Boudreaux had come back
from the Great War a hero like his ancestor, crossed with
sashes and decorations from Belgium and France, each
almost mad with pleasure at the notion of decorating an
American who spoke French and bore a recognizable sur-
name. But he had had a single son, no more, to raise as
carefully as another man might have collected Limoges
porcelain—only to see him take to the sky in the 1930s and
make an independent living dusting crops through the
southwest parishes, hurling his patched biplane over cotton
fields from dawn to dusk as if he were determined to destroy the Colonel's pleasure. But it appeared the Old Man's
will had sustained him, and Lance Boudreaux II had survived three crashes in order to enter the Army Air Corps in

1940 and rise to the rank of Colonel himself before, at last, amidst a conflagration too vast even to be managed by his father, Lance II had gone down in the winter of 1944 over the oil fields of Roumania.

Dying, the old man had called for Lance. Servants, some of them the children of West African blacks who had been brought to the Island before the turn of the century, speaking nothing but their own brand of French, swore the Old Man was calling for his son. Some, less traditionalist, had claimed he was calling for his grandson. But it made no difference. Neither could be produced. The grandson had vanished amidst the turmoil of California as surely and as finally as the son had vanished over Ploesti. So that Mr. Landry had sat there during the final hours, being spoken to as if, at almost seventy, he were son and grandson alike, hearing what had been and what was to be, how the Island would sustain them all until the very ramparts of infinity itself were breached, and the Truth should come to relieve them of their burden.

Mr. Landry had drifted into sleep once or twice, only to be awakened by one of the blacks bringing the narcotic required by the Old Man, and a glass of fine Napoleon brandy for this lawyer, this man whose sole duty it was to remain awake, to hold to his duty till the end. The cool stare of the servant reproved him, and he had thrown down the brandy and sat straight in his chair.

He had remembered the boy. Not well, for he had been hardly more than a cipher, a presence in a distant room somewhere when the Old Man and Mr. Landry did their business. Lance III had been a curly-headed shadow, the sole remnant of his father's life, purchased, as it happened, from his mother for a price. His mother, found by Lance Boudreaux somewhere between Orange, Texas, and Lafayette, Louisiana, on one of his airborne careers across the bottom of the state. In a diner, in an auto court, in a dime store, or to put aside euphemism, in a whorehouse. His mother who had come into Mr. Landry's New Orleans office one autumn afternoon in 1954 at the invitation of Lance I, whose mansion she had left almost before Lance II had gotten across the sea, and who, for reasons buried in her heart and possibly in the soil of Roumania, had, in return for a cashier's check for $250,000, signed an authentic act by which she gave over permanent custody of her son to his grandfather, agreeing that the old man should adopt him and treat him in all particulars as if the boy were his own son, as if, in fact, there had been no generation intervening. She had smoked and read, smoked and signed. It was done, and the young Italianate man with her, most recent in a long succession—her chauffeur, someone had snickered, cause he rides her—rose, offered his arm, and guided her back to the dusty Cadillac parked downstairs.

   — Did you want to see him . . . before . . . ? Mr. Landry had asked her. — You see, there are no visiting rights . . . not ever . . .

   She had paused for a moment, as if she did not understand what he was saying, what he was asking her. — See him? He's dead . . . isn't he?

   — No . . . I mean his . . . your son.

   — Oh. No. I saw him. Last Christmas. He looks like Lance. Exactly like Lance. He'll die, too. You watch. You can't depend on them. The act like gods, nothing can hurt them. Then, when they get you to believing it, they go and die. No, I don't want to see the son of a bitch. . . .

   She had gone to Houston, then, had lived in a suite at the Shamrock Hotel for four years in what Mr. Landry had been given to understand was a state of sybaritic luxury and perpetual unrelieved drunkenness, hiring and discharging chauffeurs one after another, having, on occasion, more than one at a time, buying extra cars to justify them if not to anyone else, at least to herself, not because morality was at

issue, but because of the extravagance so shameful to a girl
from a South Louisiana diner, auto court, or even whorehouse. Until one evening, full of Black Jack and Nembutals,
she had fallen or leapt ten stories onto a lower roof and
bounced, broken and bloody, into the swimming pool to bob
there, a shambles of ruined meat, amidst hysterical guests
of the hotel who, no soberer than she, could not fathom this
thing in the water which had invaded their evening's pleasure and floated there before them, draining red fluid into
the scented water, semblance and prophecy of last things.
Her most recent chauffeur had left her, it seemed, and her
money had run out. But Mr. Landry, who had a long recall,
was never sure it had not been an older and deeper wound
that had sent her spiraling down out of the sky into the
oil-rich of Houston even as Lance II had gone down into
the oil of Roumania.

Fourier had finished his stuffed grape leaves, downed the
last of the wine, and begun on his list again.

— You know, he quit Tulane, but he seems to have finished med school at UCLA. If he wanted a new life, why
do you reckon he went back to medical school all the hell
and gone out here?

Mr. Landry gestured to the moustached waiter for more
wine. It was absurd. He was mildly drunk, but he did so
anyhow, and saw a grin of anticipation appear on the face
of the Turk or Greek or whatever he was. As the wine
flowed, the tip mounted. Mr. Landry smiled back at him.
It was the only normal, calculable response he had seen since
landing at the San Francisco International Airport. — La
vita nuova, Mr. Landry heard himself mutter.

— How's that, sir, young Fourier asked.

— Everybody wants a new life, Mr. Landry said. — Only
what they really want is the old life. Once more. To do
better.

Young Fourier's face was flushed. He was beginning to feel his liquor. — Shit, you know, that's true . . .

Mr. Landry did not smile. He stared at Fourier. Even a man taken in drink should control his language better. An attorney in New Orleans, at least one connected with a good firm, did not use such speech. Not even in his sleep. Conclusions might be drawn.

The wine came, and it was cold and tart, the resin adding a fresh element to the old flavor of decent, not excellent, white wine. That was why they added it to the wine, the ancients. Not to preserve, but to enhance.

Mr. Landry remembered Lance's room—no, rooms, really, in his grandfather's mansion on the Island. Like a pawnshop, Mr. Landry had thought. Rooms filled with books; records; equipment; laboratory supplies; musical instruments; film projectors; a heap of cameras, including Rolleis, a speed graphic, a Leica; rakes; spades; oyster knives; rifles; shotguns of every gauge; a rack of pistols, including black powder weapons, Colt's Navy, Remington Army; reproductions of paintings from every conceivable period nailed to the wall in and out of frame, including a Rousseau which might well not have been a reproduction; three-dimensional chess sets; television monitors; uniforms of armies current and long disbanded; flags from nations no longer in existence; bundles of periodicals ranging from the *Yellow Book* to *Acta Chemica*, journals representing every imaginable profession and interest; tents; and uninflated life rafts; cracked wooden Buddhas; archaeological rubbish from the pre-Columbian period of the Americas and from Sumer and Akkad; canteens; axes; magnifying glasses; retorts; microscopes; and a great chart of the zodiac which almost covered one wall, its corners pinned down by enlarged photos of Proust and Rommel, an Indian Swami of uncertain identity, and Artie Shaw—all this and so much more. There was a coin collection, including U.S. gold pattern coins which had never been issued. There were stamp albums and envelopes full of bank notes from failed countries, bottles filled with Formalin in which there floated and bobbed the decayed ruins of two-headed kingsnakes, large worms from the Amazon, and an embryo of something like a pig or an ape which, heedless of gravity, hovered like a tiny dancer, its something like a mouth caught in a permanent leer, its unfinished limbs swaying amidst the cloudy fluid, filled with a faint golden dust composed, it seemed, of cells from the thing itself.

But Mr. Landry could not, for the life of him, place amidst this recollected clutter the face of Lance Boudreaux III. He could, in memory, see there sprawled between a large crate of clay pigeons and a lithography stone, the figure of a small boy sitting cross-legged above a board of some kind, a shiny instrument in his hand, and to one side a large leather-bound book obviously older than the Boudreaux holdings themselves, in some strange language, its print large, some passages in red. Mr. Landry remembered looking down, his eyes still sharp in those days, seeing just these words: *O Diabolus, Dominus Mundi, ad Servus Tuum, Veniat . . .*

He had thought little of it. The Latin, after all, was not strange to him. He had served mass from his tenth to his seventeenth year and could recite the ordinary of the mass, his part and the priest's, without a falter. As it happened, he did not know what all the words meant, and Father Briscoe had suggested that he not bother to learn, as it might confuse him.

Still he had known what those words meant. What he could not bring to mind was the board, and whether anything was on it. Nor could he remember the boy's face. All he could conjure up was a pair of green eyes and a strange distant sound in the background, something over a local radio station with the improbable title, "Thermopylae."

— By God, it's . . . Jerry Garcia, young Fourier said.
— Look.

The street band had come closer now, and the one Fourier had noticed looked much like all the rest, bearded, a little rotund, long unkempt hair, work clothes, a guitar clutched to his belly. He paused in front of The Forum, smiled a beatific smile. The young people around clapped.
— This is for Lance, he grated, — wherever, whenever. The One Who Stands . . . Then he began to sing and the others, hirsute, pallid, grasping a variety of instruments, joined in.

The Turk brought baklava, and young Fourier whispered that they could use one more bottle of the retsina. The waiter looked at Fourier and then at Mr. Landry. Could they manage yet another? No, Mr. Landry thought, but goddamn the Turks. He nodded soberly. One more. As he walked away, Mr. Landry tried to make out the lyrics of the song. Something about out of the earth, out of the earth, the soul of the earth, the soul of the earth, the soul of forever. The wine came then, along with the baklava. They ate the dessert, paid the bill and left tip enough so that the waiter paid no mind when they rose carrying not only the bottle of wine with its cheap paper label, but the two glasses as well.

They walked back to the Carleton Hotel then, Mr. Landry taking care, walking slowly, a little unsteady, looking into the windows of the bookshops, headshops, small restaurants specializing in natural food where he could buy a bowl of brown rice for twenty-five cents, complete with a pair of chopsticks which broke in two when you drew them from their cheap paper wrappers. There was Robbie's Chinese walk-in, and a place that specialized in hot dogs of various kinds. There was a newsstand on the corner near the campus with copies of *Rolling Stone*, *Crawdaddy*, and other papers dedicated to music and nature and how to build a cabin in the Sierras or the Rockies without help and without nails.

The hotel was quiet, its lobby dark. Only the desk area was lighted, and as they passed to go to the tiny elevator, Mr. Landry thought he saw figures reclining in the lobby, on sofas, chairs, and even on the floor. There was only the night clerk awake, his eyes wide and fixed on a telephone switchboard without lights, a cigarette caught between his teeth, and the sweet distant stench of smoke which young Fourier identified as that of extremely fine dope.

When he reached his room, Mr. Landry expected that he would fall asleep quickly that night. But it was not so.

Instead, as he lay down, he found himself standing in subdued sunlight, under a live oak tree. Before him, in the cool morning glow, between rows of blooming gardenias, were open French doors and a terrace with a small fountain. Mr. Landry could hear music coming from beyond the doors. A Mozart sonata.

He stood for a long moment, breathing deeply. By God, Mr. Landry thought, not here. Even dreaming. Even drinking too much for the first time in forty years. I don't want to be here, because even now, so old that the very memory of love seems an embarrassment, I can't stand it. I would rather dream of hell, Milton's flames and Dante's ice, than remember what I have not thought of in almost thirty years.

But nothing changed. He was still there, in the courtyard of the house where they had lived when they were first married. The music stopped, and he heard her voice continuing the melody, low, crystalline, close by. He had wanted to think the sonata came from a phonograph, but he realized that then they had had no phonograph. There had only been the piano brought from Mandeville, from her father's summer place across the lake. Later there would be a phonograph, and music from it in the morning before the sun broke through the trees. He would put on Albinoni or one of the Marcellos, or perhaps Vivaldi before she woke. He would brew the strong rich coffee and chicory which they ground and mixed themselves, and set two cups on the linen cloth draped fresh each morning on the metal and glass table at the shaded end of the terrace. And when the sun's first light touched the peak of the fountain, he would go into the bedroom, lean down and kiss her, waking her gently, bringing her back into this pendant world they shared, knowing that nothing in it mattered so much as her presence, her smile, her love.

Then they would sit on the terrace and talk until the sun touched the edge of the cloth and he rose to gather up his papers and walk down to St. Charles Avenue where the trolley ran. Only in the depths of winter was that ritual broken, or on those mornings when rain drove them into the breakfast room.

He was still standing, it seemed, in the back of the yard near the old brick wall covered with English ivy. He walked toward the terrace then, toward that melody he had not heard in so many years, knowing that he would not get through the open doors because, even dreaming, that was too much to hope for, and that never before in the years intervening, since that last morning they had spent on the terrace had he found her image again as he slept. He thought, because if I could walk through those doors, there is nothing in the universe, given that I could see her face, which could draw me out again. I would die there, go to hell there, and laugh at the cost, saying how can you scare off a man who has not cared whether he lived or died in thirty years, who has had nothing to wake up for but the bitter law in thirty years? As if, God forbid, death were something other than an end to life, indeed rather the terminus of all things, beyond which nothing lay at all.

By then, it seemed, he was on the terrace, that previous voice so close that he knew she must be sitting just within the shadow of the doors, on the piano bench sorting through her music, searching for something to follow the Mozart, most likely one of Bach's inventions. He remembered then, not the day but the epoch. It was 1938, the spring. He was doing well. Not as well as he would do later, but well. She was not pregnant then, would not be for months yet. But she would be in the fall of 1939, and that pregnancy for which she had hoped and prayed would silence the music for all time, leaving not even a child behind. Nothing but pain. He stepped hopelessly into the dark doorway, turned.

And found himself blinking into pale sunlight falling through the blinds of the room. He looked around the faded walls covered with cracking wallpaper. The woodwork, varnished many times, was dark with age and scarred by the transient blows of generations of baggage and bellmen. Strange what the sun does to whatever it touches, searing away the blur of the commonplace, individuating each scar and crease, setting apart that thing as standing forth in itself alone.

Mr. Landry rose slowly from his bed and walked over to the washbowl beside the windows. The mirror was in shadow so he switched on the weak naked bulb above. He saw his face then, and a spear of shock thrilled him. Awakening from the terrace, from the mild New Orleans spring morning long ago, he had almost forgotten. I am nearly seventy now, he thought, looking at the spare controlled wizened face that had not belonged to him on such a morning long ago, which had only lurked then in the well of possibility, presuming the practice did not kill him, in case he survived the loss, the winter afternoons and interminable evenings alone. In case he was unfortunate enough to extend his life across time, missing each likely chance to die until he came at last to stand behind this ancient alien face that she had never seen, would, by the grace of God, never know.

I'm even older than that, he thought, shaving slowly, carefully, with a straight razor she had given him that last anniversary they had been together. It shone in the pallid sunlight, its edge honed deep into the heavy body of the steel. He had used it for over thirty years and more, as if to do other might be to deny the meaning, the magnitude of his loss. I'm so old that I can't hold it off any more. Only a little while to go, and it's catching up with me. As if dying were no more than the sum of things you love rushing up from behind, overcoming you, rescuing you from time.

He began to dress. He had control of himself now, and he did not think how many times he would be willing to die in order to enter those French doors two thousand miles and thirty years away, to turn and find her there, three, five years into their marriage, leafing through her music, suddenly looking up surprised, saying

— René, do you know the time?

Yes. He knew. The summer of 1938. On State Street and sometime past eight in the morning. Almost time for him to be downtown in those oak-lined, book-filled caverns where the minor keys of his life were scored and played out.

Down on Telegraph Avenue, he could already hear music and see people moving though the sun had barely risen high enough to touch the street. They looked as if they were dressed in rags. Women wearing loose ugly dresses and shawls over their heads. Men wearing cloth caps and cheap coats and ragged pants. He remembered Prague just after the war, but he could not remember that the sun ever shone. The people there had dressed like these, had moved like ghosts or sleepwalkers amidst the tumbled ruins of their city and their lives. But they had had no choice. Something alien had invaded their lives. Das Dritte Reich, a demonic vision separated entirely from reality. It had come upon them, and when finally it had dissipated, there was another vicious dream to take its place.

He shook his head, staring downward. But why do these children pretend? Why do they act as if they were the remnant left over, the human particles somehow not claimed by the holocaust? Jesus, he thought, it doesn't take artillery, does it? It doesn't take the Nazis. It takes no more than the destruction of the soul. In Prague there had been music, too. Street music. A blind violinist sitting on a box next to the broken wall of the gutter railway station. Before him on the shattered pavement lay his cap with a few coins in it and on his chest, on the lapel of a frayed suit coat which did not match his pants was a beautiful ribbon with a military decoration hanging from it. He played only two or three songs, but Mr. Landry remembered how strange it seemed that one of them was "I'll See You Again," as if out of his darkness the violinist chose to mock the visible world and all that it purported to contain by mocking himself.

II

Young Fourier knocked. He was casually dressed, without a tie, his hair fluffed up as if he had not combed it. He noticed Mr. Landry's long inquisitory look. He smiled what Mr. Landry supposed he considered an ingratiating smile.

— When in California, young Fourier laughed. Mr. Landry walked to the elevator. On the way down, he studied the list of faculty members they were scheduled to meet with while Fourier studied a map of the campus. The lobby was empty now, and a new clerk was behind the desk.

Just outside, there was a newspaper rack, and the headline of the *San Francisco Tribune* howled BAY HORROR KILLINGS.

It seemed that in a nearby suburb south of the peninsula, in a place called Daly City police had discovered the bodies of a number of people hideously murdered, as if according to some ritual. The body of one young woman had been cut almost in two. There was evidence that she had been in an advanced stage of pregnancy, but no fetus had been found.

Mr. Landry almost dropped the paper. He wondered sometimes if these things actually happened, or if there was a stable of demented journalists somewhere paid California-size salaries to conceive of the most incredible degeneracies that diseased and fevered minds could invent. But he knew better. In the firm there was one young attorney whose lot it was to handle such criminal litigation as could not in conscience and good business be avoided. He had casually told Mr. Landry enough of his own experiences to convince. The story in the paper was doubtless true. For a fleeting moment, Mr. Landry wondered which of his sins might be the specific one for which he had been condemned to live into this generation.

He threw the paper into a receptacle as they began to walk toward Sather Gate. Along the way, students seemed to be everywhere, handing out leaflets of one kind or another. Some supported, some attacked, but all were written in a dialect only approximating English, and each one howled a Great Outrage, a Crowning Act too Loathsome to be Borne.

— They really get steamed up, young Fourier observed, steering Mr. Landry toward the cafeteria.

— But it's all the same, Mr. Landry said, peering through the handful of urgent messages that had been pressed upon him. — Support the Farm Workers' Union, don't buy table grapes, free Huey Newton, open admissions and no tests for minorities, abortion at state expense, or we will bring down the social order. What is anyone supposed to make of that?

— It's all nonnegotiable, Fourier allowed, his eyes crinkling as the first shafts of sunlight reached the broad cool plaza.

— Ummm, Mr. Landry smiled approvingly. — Nothing is nonnegotiable . . . except . . .

— They don't have that out here, Fourier said quickly. — Everyone is too young to . . .

Mr. Landry nodded. He looked around as they entered the cafeteria line. Fourier was right. It wasn't surprising to see so many young people on a campus, but he could not remember seeing anyone much over thirty since the plane had set down across the bay. Toyland. An adolescent fantasy.

As they ate their eggs, Mr. Landry mused. — I wonder why young Boudreaux would have come . . .

— Here? Didn't you say he was . . . weird?

— Ummm. He wasn't . . . I never said . . . weird. Out of the ordinary.

— Sir, every spook and freak and stranger in the country is tuned in here. It's the music and the politics and . . . everything. It's where it's at.

— You mean, where it is.

— Whatever. But if Mr. Boudreaux's grandson was . . . out of the ordinary, he'd . . . this is weirdsville, sir. There's not a normal person within ten miles of us right now. Skin-freaks, dope-freaks, bomb-freaks . . . these people do anything they want.

Fourier looked around. At the next table, two blond girls in shorts and halters were eating and talking rapidly. Mr. Landry had the notion that both were attractive by the standard of the time, allowing for the fact that they were barefoot, hair uncombed, breasts almost exposed in the loose halters, and the shorts so closely cut that one of the girls, when she moved her legs, exposed a portion of pubic hair. Mr. Landry was not shocked. He had visited zoos before. However worthy animals might be, they did not clothe themselves, and some of their personal habits were coarse. As he regarded them, one of the girls was saying to the other,

— . . . told me, you want an ace in Math 390, you got to give head. That's it, honey. You know any chick with an ace in there, you know she's been down . . .

Young Fourier blushed. Mr. Landry turned away, understanding only the syntax and grammar. The words meant nothing at all.

— This is the heart of the beast, Fourier was saying, as he threw down the last of his bad coffee quickly and picked up his tray.

They walked through Sather Gate into the academic campus, and on toward a low building done in some style only to be described as a California view of Spanish colonial. Inside it was cool and subdued. At a desk a young woman with olive skin, burning dark eyes, and a peculiar accent spoke softly into a phone and told them that Professor Khaldoun would see them.

The office door was deep scarlet color, and on it Mr. Landry and Fourier saw the lovely swirls and rises of Arabic script. Underneath, in small roman letters it was declared that here stayed Professor Khaldoun, professor of Middle Eastern thought. Below that was pasted a crudely mimeographed broadsheet which declared the unyielding determination of the Palestinian people to recapture their homeland. And, incidentally, to scourge from the face of the earth those who had usurped it.

They knocked and entered, in time to see Professor Khaldoun face down on a small carpet, a shaft of sunlight embracing him. He completed some formula in which he was involved, and rose quickly, smiling, to greet them.

— You will pardon me, he said in excellent English. — It must be done. You are the lawyer Landry from New Orleans?

Mr. Landry bowed, offered his card, and pumped hands with Professor Khaldoun in that peculiar fashion he had learned from distant French kin, which was the style almost everywhere but in America.

— You come about Lancelot, Professor Khaldoun said musingly, as he moved a small table behind a cluttered desk, and began to prepare cups of strong dark coffee.

— Yes, Mr. Landry began, staring along with Fourier at the process, almost unable to wait for the thick aromatic brew after the nasty stuff they had had in the cafeteria.

— Your letter said his grandfather . . . was no more?

— Passed on, Mr. Landry answered in a similar hushed tone. It is of the essence of advocates that they be able to take on at once the color of the place where they must work. It is not a conscious thing, or it would be useless. It is an inherent capacity by which he who would preserve or alter the status of a situation in which he is alien shifts his cognitions into the key dominant amongst the contenders with whom he deals.

— Allah, may His name be praised, is just. So be it.

— Amen, Fourier said almost mechanically. Mr. Landry did not look at him. It fitted nicely and was to be expected. Fourier's family, originally from Breauxville, was Baptist and of a peculiarly demonstrative sect given to baptisms in the bayou and penitential utterances on Wednesday evenings so loud that passing Catholics were chilled at the sound of booming declarations of the most intimate personal failings, as if someone had put their own whispered confessions on an amplified loudspeaker.

— And by that passage of his ancestor, Lancelot has become rich . . . ?

Mr. Landry's expression did not alter. He was used to greed by proxy. — He has become universal legatee to a considerable estate . . .

The professor placed steaming coffee before each of them and sat down. He smiled indulgently.

— A considerable estate. By the standards of your South, I am sure.

Mr. Landry's eyes narrowed. — A considerable estate. By Saudi Arabian standards, I should think.

The professor's eyes widened. — Land?

— An island, and perhaps 6,000 acres of the richest farmland in Louisiana. There is also a lagoon, and a number of servitudes on adjacent estates.

Professor Khaldoun spread his hands. — What can I tell you?

He told them a great deal. He told them of a tall, bearded, green-eyed young man with a silver star emblazoned on his forehead, whether by tattooing or some other means he could not say. He said that this Lancelot, who never used any other name, had appeared before him at the end of a quarter, had demanded, under university regulations, to take the final examination in a graduate seminar on late medieval Islamic thought, and had, before the professor's eyes, completed the nine-part examination in less than an hour.

— When he handed me the papers, he said I was wise, and it was good to contend with me before Allah, may His blessings embrace us. And when I looked at the papers, he had written the examination in Arabic.

Moreover, because of this wonder, the professor had followed Lancelot's doings thereafter, had even gone to hear the opening of his band at the Hungry i, a club in San Francisco reserved for only the most immediately popular rock bands. There he had heard the peculiar rhythms and eastern melodies of Lance's group—but most strange, the lyrics.

— I cannot remember to quote, he told them. — But names
like "I talk to the sword," "Doom at the bottom of your
cup." That one, it was about poisoning. It said he had come
from a violent place, a place where men were connoisseurs
of guns and knives, a barbarous place. But that he sought
a place without violence, where all contention was settled
without the shedding of blood. Where those who could not
exist together would vie with poison—poisoned food and
drink, poisoned garments, poison in flowers, in rings,
poisoned letter-paper, vials of poison gas in autos. And there
was this terrible refrain,

> Belladonna, deadly nightshade,
> make again music that once was made,
> Angel of death, dark as the sea,
> prey upon those who pray not for me.

— Is this what is taught in New Orleans, Professor Khaldoun asked.
— No, Mr. Landry said. — No. I think not.
— The juju, young Fourier began.
— Jews, the professor mused. — It is not surprising. The
Kabbalah. They are a venomous people. Their ways . . . but
of course you know . . .
Mr. Landry rose abruptly, thanked the professor, telling
him that there were others that must be seen. They held
each other's eyes for a long moment. Then the professor
shrugged. — He last came here after obtaining his doctor of
medicine degree. He had already degrees in physics and
philosophy. That time he was clean-shaven, indeed, his head
was shaven, and the star was gone. He wore a caste mark
where it had been. We talked. He said that he embraced the
cause of all those who had lost what nothing else could
be substituted for . . . that he would be the physician of the
world.
— You understood . . .

The professor's eyes flashed. — Of course, I understood . . .

Mr. Landry was astonished to see tears in the professor's eye. — He will give back to the bereaved their lost homeland . . .

Fourier and Mr. Landry exchanged glances as they walked back into the outer office where the sultry secretary fixed them both with her dark eyes.

— . . . and so you had better not to seek him, because . . .

Mr. Landry was astonished to find himself turning, looking at the professor as if from a great distance. — If I forget thee, O Zion . . .

— Selah, Fourier said hoarsely, and the young secretary said something in a harsh vicious whisper in no language either of them understood.

— Deny him his inheritance, they heard the professor cry after them, his voice muffled by the partitions and the distance down the dimly lit hallway, — keep it from him, or perish with your kind. He is Lancelot, a true Christian, a hater of those whom all Christians hate . . . a true . . .

III

Professor Hellstrom awaited them in his office. Mr. Landry approved of him at once. The office looked like a monk's cell. There was no desk, only a table, three chairs, and a blackboard covered with that peculiar arcana of the physicist which had shaken the world more profoundly than all the pother of Hegel, the ranting of Marx. Young Fourier was amazingly subdued as they entered the office. He held Professor Hellstrom's hand for a long moment.

— I . . . never thought . . . to meet you, sir . . .

Hellstrom was a man of middle height, deeply tanned, his eyes almost hidden by thick glasses. He smiled broadly. — You do physics, son?

— I did . . . in college. Enough to know that . . . nothing is like it was before you . . .

— I ain't Einstein, son. Just an old East Texas boy who got through Sam Houston State in math . . .

— . . . and shared a Nobel prize for tensor analysis of photon vectors . . .

— I should have been a metaphysician, the professor laughed.

— You are, Fourier said, and subsided.

Mr. Landry felt uncomfortable. He did not grudge Fourier his knowledge, his capacity to evaluate, however crudely, the work of another. He only wished he had done as much. He said nothing. Only watched the two of them as the professor lit a long slim cigar and offered one to Fourier.

— You got one hell of a young lawyer here, Mr. Landry, Hellstrom said. — You know that?

— I didn't know it, Mr. Landry said honestly. — I'm beginning to.

— Don't a lawyer have to be able to see into things? He's got to take on as may roles as there are, doesn't he?

— I think he does. All things to all men.

— He knows all you need to know about what I do, Hellstrom said, leaning his ladderback chair against the wall. — I wish my goddamn genius graduate students knew as much. Hell, Lance knew it. That's how he walked in here, did himself a Ph.D. in S matrix theory in a year and half and walked away. Shit, he raped the goddamned department, you know?

— Sir?

— Tunneling theory. He did some equations that would make God cry for the sheer beauty of them. Take a look at this.

Professor Hellstrom slammed his chair to the floor, grabbed up a piece of chalk and a rag, and began to scrawl equations across the chalkboard with one hand as he erased with the other. — This is what he did. Described how the proton world-line has to be calculated outside any dimensional structure, how virtual particle exchange is no sort of exchange at all. Look.

More equations. Fourier leaned forward. Mr. Landry sat back. Professor Hellstrom wrote faster and faster. — Son of a bitch, take at look at this.

— No time coordinates, Fourier said.

— That's because exchange doesn't happen in time. All determinable dimensions are consistent. Do you understand?

— Then, there is no pion exchange in I-space . . .

— Wrong. There is. The nucleon is defined variously as proton or neutron depending upon the positionality of the pion. But not dimensionally. The exchange is not a physical event. It's a mental event, and that goddamned Louisiana coonass figured how to set it out . . .

— That's . . . Nobody . . . , Fourier began.

— Right. It's all a crock, Hellstrom said. — Except for one little old thing. The son of a bitch set out equations that fit the data. Nobody believes they mean anything. Shit, when I back off, neither do I. But now and then, just once in a while . . .

— He joined physical and mental events. In a unified mathematical field.

— Yeah, that's what I think he did. But the bastards in this department . . . bunch of goddamned positivists. Proof doesn't mean a damned thing to them. Logical rigor, beauty, that damned perfection of something that works straight out, upside down, or sideways—they don't give a damn. Listen, if I hadn't had that damned piece of gold from Stockholm, they'd of told Lance to go take him a degree in astrology . . . the finest mind since Niels Bohr . . . and these dumb bastards . . . they're looking for the next transuranic element. As if Glenn Seabourg hasn't given us enough of those damned phantoms.

— Do you know where he is, Mr. Landry put in. — We have to find him.

— Ain't that the damnedest thing? Hellstrom winked at Fourier. — All this and a bundle of money, too. Naw, I don't know. All I know is this damned school had the best mind in thirty years, and all these cretins in physics wanted to do was burn him at the stake. Listen, there's people in this department would like to put out a contract on Feinmann . . . You don't know what it's like. Some of these guys come to colloquiums and quote Einstein: God doesn't play dice with the universe.

— That's nonsense, Mr. Landry said. — Of course He does. It's His universe, isn't it?

Professor Hellstrom sat down at his table. From somewhere he pulled forth a bottle of Jack Daniels. — Youall don't know what a relief it is to sit down with sensible men. You bet your sweet ass He does. Lance said, this cosmos, the choirs of heaven and the furniture of earth is His entertainment. He whiles away eons in loving play, and this pendant universe shall sum zero, ending like a great prelude and fugue, everything coming out.

— Right, Mr. Landry said. — Praise be His name.

— Right, Professor Hellstrom repeated. — I tell you this: Lance *knew*. Physics ain't just experiment and reasoning any more, you know. It's . . . something else. Lance used to say, go listen to Bach. Put on the Second French Suite for harpischord. Number is all. You remember what Paul Dirac did? Pure mind. Pure insight. Let the goddamned experimentalists fool around in the mud. Kids like to make mud pies. But it's mind. Pure mind. If I can set out the positron in my mind, if it's rigorously correct, if it's beautiful . . . then it's true. Because . . .

— What we do in the mind is more than just. . . . , Fourier began excitedly.

— Right, Hellstrom cut him off. — It's the only truth. The world is a place we have in the mind . . . the only world there is. Lance knew. The last time he came by, he told me. He said, I have put down the darkness. I mean to bring the light. I am the one who stands . . .

— Is there somewhere we might look for him? Mr. Landry asked.

— Sure, Professor Hellstrom grinned. — Somewhere in the dimensional structure of our world. He hasn't figured out yet how to be free of it. In his mind he knows . . . but . . .

— Yes?

— He's still made of meat. But if anyone can break free, he's the one. Lance is . . . he understands . . .

IV

They walked back the way they had come then. It was close to noon. Students poured out of the classroom buildings, and they saw workmen putting up audio equipment near the stairs of the administration building. Blacks with absurd hairdos, intense young men with thick glasses, women with broad shoulders, all were gathered watching grimly as the loudspeakers were set in place. Down toward the end of the walk, where Telegraph Avenue struck the purlieus of the campus, half a dozen pushcarts had drawn up, and students were buying hot dogs, burritos, or brown rice with sambals from hairy proprietors. Mr. Landry and Fourier chose the brown rice, a health food, according to the placard on the side of the cart. It was nice and strong and they put soy sauce on it and ate it with chopsticks, squatting there at the mouth of Telegraph, looking down its length in the glare of sun from a cloudless sky, able to see almost a mile, utterly unlike the humid Louisiana noontime when clouds were building toward thunderheads and the moisture spread a haze over everything not immediate and close at hand.

As they ate, a man came out and placed a box on the
pavement close to them. He was the epitome of rednecks.
Fourier shook his head and Mr. Landry watched him
closely. They wondered if he could be from California with
that red hair, that face like a side of aged beef covered
with freckles. As they watched, students began to gather
around, laughing, speaking to him in good humor.

— Hey, Hubert, where you at? What's the good news,
Hubert?

The man smiled back at them, drew some of them close
and spoke to them earnestly. From under his nylon jacket
he drew a tattered book, struck it with his hand, driving
home some point he deemed important.

— Must have stolen it from the Gideons, young Fourier
observed. — See?

— He looks like someone from Shreveport, Mr. Landry
said. — Or Plain Dealing. Or Oil City.

— He's fixing to preach, Mr. Landry, young Fourier said.

Mr. Landry rose to his feet, aware for the first time that
he had been sitting on the grass in his business suit. With
his Dobbs hat on. Something in the air, he thought. Maybe
if we could just get all these poor devils to Texas, they'd
be all right. Maybe they ought to declare California unfit
for human habitation.

He was dusting pollen and grass off his pants when he
heard, over Hubert's breathless, excited nasal drone, another
round of applause. He looked up to see another box being
placed on the pavement some ten or fifteen feet from where
Hubert was preaching. But the young man setting up the
box was astonishing. He was tall, hair long and twisted in
contorted bundles like the locks of a gorgon. His face bore
an unchanging expression somehow both sneer and tri-
umphant smile at once. He wore a set of evening dress
clothes, complete with white tie and tails, so old as to have
lost its smooth blackness and turned a dark green, the color

of patina on an ancient coin. He wore a tophat and a long cloak of a hue not quite matching the suit. His formal shirt was filthy, and in place of cufflinks Mr. Landry saw he had twisted paperclips to hold his cuffs together.

He worked with feverish speed. When the box was set up, he draped it with a piece of seedy scarlet velvet. Then, down on his hands and knees, he scratched out a pentagram with a piece of charcoal, placing indecipherable initials in the five points of the star.

— I don't believe it, Young Fourier was saying. — Do you believe it?

— I'm looking at it, Mr. Landry said. — I guess I *have* to believe it.

By then, Hubert had noticed the new arrival. He stopped in midsentence and watched the young man jump to the top of the box, lift his arms above his head, and scream out in a voice of amazing volume and power, — Satanas diabolus, here in the blaze of noonday, here at the end of the Western world, come to us, bless us, send us your power and confusion, grant us chaos, and slaughter us all—dead, dead, dead . . .

Cheers from some of the students who had been listening to Hubert, and who now moved to encircle the tall boy, who swirled his cape, twisted his body, and uttered short, piercing squeals like those of a trapped bat.

— Some prayer, Fourier observed. — How the hell can you get an audience with stuff like that? Who wants to die?

— O God of Israel, God of Abraham and David, cast down the infidel, the unbeliever, Hubert intoned as if it was a formula he had used often before.

The young man turned on him, laughing exultantly.
— That's him, he howled. — You invoke him, too. The one you call God is Satanas, creator of the world, enemy of the pleroma, hater of the uncreated . . .

— O God of Moses, Hubert began.

— God of Moses, the young man echoed, — send us the doom reserved for the gentiles. Let us know of you by way of your judgment on us. O God of the festivals and lights, God of the popes and emperors, God whose madness and cruelty is the model for all mankind, God whose whores and pathics are everywhere, God who crucified him who came, the New Anthropos—bless the tongue of this prophet, and let his mouth run with blood. Teach him blasphemy, and show him how to kill . . .

Fourier had been speaking to a long-haired girl standing nearby. — She says it goes on like this almost every day. She says last Good Friday was something else. . . . The nut in the tuxedo was crying out for the death of Anthropos, whoever the hell that is, and Hubert was crying for the blessing of innocence in the blood of the lamb. Said it started to rain, and Hubert called it grace. The other nut called it blood.

Hubert paused till his antagonist at last ran out of breath. — I tell you this, he said. — I hope the Lord burns your rotten ass for a thousand years, that's what I hope . . . you goddamn commanist . . .

The students booed. Fair play for the devil. The Satanist crowed triumphantly. — You see, brothers, he curses his own God . . .

— Jesus and the Holy Spirit, put him down, Hubert howled. — Send him down to suffer with youall's enemies . . . enemies . . .

— Jesus is a joke, the young man shouted back.

— Hey, Young Fourier said, turning toward Mr. Landry just in time to see him move toward the box the cloaked young man was standing on and, with a single hard kick, upend him, sending him sprawling into the rice cart, overturning it too and causing confusion among the scattered long-haired students. — Go it, Hubert yelled. — See, the Lord answers; the Lord provides; now don't he . . . ?

Young Fourier pushed two haltered sunbleached blonds aside, grabbed Mr. Landry, and began walking rapidly across the street, down Telegraph, toward Dwight Way.
— I want one of them big hot dogs down the street, he said in a controlled conversational tone.
— That miserable bastard, Mr. Landry said, to the astonishment of Fourier, — taking our Lord's name in vain.
— Well, Fourier said, his pace increasing, — I know what you mean, sir. Bunch of perverts . . . whole state full of 'em.
The perverts, at last having gathered themselves together, headed up behind the young man. His cloak was befouled with rice, and behind him, looming like an omen, was Hubert singing out praise on him who had brought the godless low and walked in grace before his God.
— Listen, we could let that hot dog go. I mean, we got a lot of places to go . . .
— Go with God, Hubert cried after them, eyes and arms aimed heavenward. The young man in the cloak and those who followed had stopped now, as if the love of evil caused short-windedness.

V

It was a hovel. She lay inside on what Mr. Landry called a pallet. Fourier squinted, his eyes watered from incense.
— Yes, when he came out of the swamp, when he came here, he was just wanting everything, wanting to get shut of whatever it was back there. He said that in July all over the island when the peppers bloomed you could smell the heat, smell the mud, the rot in the swamps. It was a paradise of heat and moisture, no matter what way you turned. Birds, egrets—what he called water turkeys, gulls. The sky full if you shouted across the water. Listen, I don't know. All I know is what he told me. What do I know about all that swamp crap? He told me that in the evening he would go down to the water and watch the bugs rising, the fish

hitting at them, the moonflowers opening for their single
night of blooming, the birds calling out of sleep, as if even
having wings was no caution against bad dreams. And the
nutria and the muskrats and the snakes. Oh, Christ, the
whole island was alive. The soil, the water, the trees, the
plants in the bayous—there wasn't anything at rest. And he
was alone in the middle of that, his father had gone down,
his mother too, and that old man not caring about anything
but sending the message on. What message? Oh, God only
knows. Some kind of crazy southern thing. How can I tell
you? You ought to know. You're from it, both of you,
aren't you? Anyhow, we met at Gillie's the first night. Gillie
the head. From Charleston or Atlanta. Working in physics
until they caught him standing on line in front of the
Van de Graaff accelerator. No hair after that. Eyes almost
gone. Had gone into the rad lab on an acid trip, looking
for the substrate, the Boundless from which all arises and to
which all returns. His fingers and toes started to go later.
Something was wrong with the blood, so he couldn't even
play lead anymore, only slap out rhythm. Nothing but nubs,
see. But Gillie told him it was worth it, that he'd seen the
God of Dirac and all his works. Jesus, I should have known
right then, you know? But we stayed listening to Gillie
and that funny spade broad who read him *I Ching* and *The
Journal of Physical Letters* everyday. She was juju. Came
from some godforsaken island, Haiti, Martinique. Someplace
where they do magic, you know. When the pain started
making Gillie scream, and even smack didn't help, she'd
whisper to him and he'd laugh and they'd go into some
dance. She called it smoke trance. Said she could bring back
the dead with it, that they'd be zombies, but that was all
right because all the whites she knew were already zombies,
though she couldn't figure out how since nobody but her
knew the smoke trance. Said she could keep Gillie alive,
even with all those pieces of forever lodged in him. What?

Yeah, the radiation. It was tomorrow that came out of the accelerator. Said it was wrong to rush things up like that, make them come before their time, and that's why they hurt us when we conjured them. Gillie used to argue with her, said we needed to get on. She'd say, all in good time, fool. They know about good time all over this prison, man. So when we left Gillie's, it was almost dawn. You want to go to my place, I said, till you find a place. Naw, he said. Here's what I want you to do. Take me to the ocean. I want to see it when the first light comes. It's not much, I said. The sun comes up on the other side. You can only see sunset on this ocean. He laughed, and we got in his Land-Rover, this big thing like a jeep full of every kind of crap you can imagine. Books, microfilms and a reader, clothes, bottles of stuff, tools, cooking gear, a guitar, but mainly books. Gillie said he would be a great physicist, only why bother, there was shorter ways. But we drove across the Golden Gate into Marin County and found this place, so when the sun rose, and the fog started burning off, he could see it spreading out, mile after mile, to the horizon. I never seen a ocean before, he said. Then he kind of looked all around. It ain't much, he said. I expected . . . something. It's only the biggest ocean in the world, I said. Yeah, I know, he told me. Ain't that a goddamn shame. I don't know; it pissed me off. I come from Sacramento, and this is the best ocean there is. This cracker was putting it down. Why don't you just go on back where you come from, I asked him. I will later, he said. My end is my beginning. Not now. Want to screw? Yes, I said. Afterward, we got this place and he went to school. You know, he signed up at Cal, and he signed up at the med school. He was taking his M.D. and this Ph.D. in physics and this degree in music theory. He started at five in the morning and kept going until one or two. Maybe four hours sleep. On the weekends he played lead with guys over at the Fillmore unless he was playing viola with the crowd of creeps in the quartet at Grace Church. And there was the poetry he wrote in class, and the music while he was eating lunch. Had this notebook with lined paper and music paper. Carried it to the toilet, kept it beside the water bed, woke up even in that four hours and scrawled things down. Like that for four years. He finished the physics and the music, but they kept giving him trouble in medicine. The residency, when he gave each patient a mantra and told the ones dying that they were and that it was good, that they had been tarrying too long, that it was time to go home. They tried to get rid of him, and he cursed the chief physician, and the next night the big shot smothered in a motel with some nurse, and they found both of them dead and naked with him on top, and they never let Lance forget. Anyhow, you know, we stayed together for four years. Everybody said, Christ, how can you stay with this guy? How can you stay with anyone so long anyhow? Gee, you know, I told them, you never screwed this guy, you never had him. Listen, you know, it was worth it. All we did was drink a lot when he was off, and take the Rover out into the country with Inglenook Cabernet and watch the sun rise and watch it set. I mean, you know, I wanted everything from him. I told him I wanted his baby. You know what? He hit me. He said anybody who wanted a baby was evil, slave of the demiurge, wanting to trap perfection in flesh, to lessen the God, to drive sparks of divinity into the darkness of life. He knocked me down, and he asked me if I was pregnant, and I said yes, and he said, you stinking whore, you're not even married. How can you be pregnant, you slut, tell me that? I said, what; he said, no. I said, don't; he said, yes. And he kicked me in the stomach and hit me with a wine bottle and somewhere along the line I zonked out, and later when I woke up, we were at Gillie's, and his woman was leaning over me and I wasn't pregnant anymore. She said, you were sick, but now you're well. Praise

Lancelot, because he knows. Praise the Great Lord who hates all ills and cures us from the sickness of life. You know what? He took me to this real cool apartment, this place near the bay, and he left this envelope and kissed me and said he couldn't take any more chances, that I had bad ways, and anyhow, he was movin' on. I said, no, you know. What will I do? You're weak, he said, you'll do just fine. Bye-bye. I cried for a long time, and I bled a lot, but later, when I got sober or whatever you get, I looked in the envelope and there was ten thousand dollars and a year's lease for the apartment in it. So I said, oh shit, it's all over anyhow, you know, and I called Kip Mendosa, and I said, hey Kippy, listen, you always dug me, you wanted me, huh? Come on to this groovy place and listen, get me a couple of bags huh? No, I know I never did. But now I want to, okay? Yeah, yeah, I can learn anything you know. Living is so bad, really, huh? Really. And I only saw him once. Saw him with some woman at the concert down in the canyon. In Strawberry Canyon. Mechanix Illustrated Celestial Dragon Dong, you know? His hair was real long, tied back. He had all these people with him, and the chick, you know, it made me want to hurt him real bad. Because she was pregnant, real pregnant, and hanging on him, you know, and he liked it. Even across half the canyon, I could tell, really. You know?

VI

It was evening again and Fourier was watching a waitress in Japanese costume as she walked quickly and gracefully toward the table, a huge tray balanced on her shoulder. It was dark now, and they sat, the three of them, in a restaurant on Fisherman's Wharf.

— ... the first time, it was something about drugs. I've got it here ...

Lieutenant Raphael riffled through pages in a file he had

brought with him. — We had a snitch lay out a little trip ol'
Lance had in mind. Down to Mexico in the Rover, and
back with ten or fifteen kilos of hash. He was going the
back way, the snitch said, across the desert, up through the
Superstitions till just above the border.

— Did you. . . ? Mr. Landry let the rest of his question
hang, as if he didn't want the answer.

Fourier's attention wandered. The Japanese waitress set
out raw fish and sauce before him. He began to eat, his eyes
holding hers. She was very beautiful, her expression smooth
and cheerful, enameled in place like her hair. Fourier wondered what it would be like to make love to a woman so
perfect, so complete. Nothing was perfect or complete
where he came from. It was wild and half made up, mad
with growth, unkempt. As she finished, smiled, and turned
away, he wondered if she was what civilization meant.

— Oh, we went after him. The whole business. Men
everywhere, choppers, close cooperation with the Mexicans.
You name it . . .

— . . . ?

— The son of a bitch drove right through us. We never
saw the Rover, and the next night they found the snitch
next to the fence at the San Diego naval base with his throat
cut and a tarot card tucked into his pocket, the hanged
man. The word was, hash dropped nine dollars a cut
that day.

— The snitch, Mr. Landry began. — Did you ever. . . ?

— Very seriously dead; not a clue. The hanged man,
Raphael said. — Seemed unnecessary. Editorial comment.

Raphael pitched into his fish. — The next time was that
business at the Four Square Gospel Tabernacle. I saw him
that time. Hell, I heard him. They broke up, you know.

— The woman he was with. . . ?

— Huh. There wasn't a woman then. Naw, she turned up
later. It was the tabernacle that broke up. It seems he came

in one Sunday, and the preacher asked for a witness. So
your boy witnessed. Held forth from nine in the morning
till four in the afternoon. By seven o'clock, they had a new
church. Church of the Living Fire. When the preacher
locked up that night, all he had left was the building, and a
few old Four Squares who couldn't hear a different drum
if you pounded it with a barge pole. There was some trouble about the building, and that's how we got involved.

— You heard him . . . preach?

— I guess that's what you call it. He talked and they
listened.

— What'd he preach about, Fourier asked, his attention
drifting back. — I mean, I thought he was . . . some kind of
hippy.

— Not that night. Naw, he had on a suit, and his hair was
cut short. Preached on the last things.

— Last things, Mr. Landry repeated, thinking for no reason of a terrace cool and pure in the rain.

— Last things, Raphael repeated, and fell silent. The waitress brought their main courses, fluffy shrimp tempura,
sukiyaki. — He said what had been, and what would be.
He told us from whence we were flung and where we're
going, what we were and what we're going to be. He . . .
started to . . .

He paused, chopsticks suspended, eyes distant. — He said
a lot of crap, Raphael finished shortly. — Impressed the
peasants, that was all.

At the end of the meal, the waitress brought green tea.
They sipped it slowly, as if it were a ceremony of their
own. — The last time, it was just an accident. The emergency room of the university hospital. We had a cop with
a magnum slug through his lungs. He was spitting blood,
and somebody called his wife down in Richmond, and I was
holding his hand, and the doctor in the emergency room was

working over him, and I heard him say, he's going to make it. The slug was AP, not a wadcutter. Nobody knows how to do anything anymore. And I looked up and it was Lance, and I damned near passed out, because you get used to seeing certain people in certain places, and this bastard you see everywhere. He looked at me and said, "Not to worry, cher; this one ain't ready to leave yet." I started to say something, but they came to take Alec to surgery, and I had to go, and I saw your boy kind of dancing down the corridor with his stethoscope waving, singing something like, *Goodbye, Joe, me gotta go, me-o, my-o* . . .

Outside, they could hear thunder over in the county. The windows of the restaurant began to mist with rain. —Did the cop . . . Fourier began.

— Oh, yeah, Raphael said. — Fine as wine. Got well, left the force. Works at City Lights Books. Reads poetry. Laid down his sword. Police shrink called it posttraumatic neurosis. Wow. Goodbye, Joe . . .

Mr. Landry gaped at the check, pushed it toward Fourier, who set his gold American Express card on top of it. The waitress' smile enlarged, as she moved away.

— Is Lance . . . I mean, do they want him . . . now? Mr. Landry asked Raphael.

Raphael studied Mr. Landry for a moment. — I don't know, he said. — I don't. Even if I did, I don't know how hard I'd look. Alec and I . . . were tight. But, down in Daly City . . . aw hell, it doesn't mean anything. There are so many spooks in this town that anything that gets done is gonna get done twice.

— What, Fourier asked. — It might be a . . . lead.

Raphael shrugged. — Down there, they had a bad killing. Bunch of heads. One girl cut up. They found it in her hand . . .

— What, Fourier asked again.

— Tarot, Raphael said. — The hanged man.

VII

— If they had a cathedral, like Notre Dame or something like that, I'd look for him there, Fourier was saying.

It was the next day, cool and clearing. The radio claimed there would be rain later. They sat on the terrace of the student union, looking out over the campus, wondering where to go next. — Or an opera house, Fourier finished.

— I think it's time we went home, Mr. Landry said. In fact, it was not the failure to find Lance Boudreaux III that depressed him. It was California. In its beauty, its almost theatrical perfection, it made him sad. It is finished, he thought. There isn't anything to be done here. California is the reward for having trekked across America, across Texas and Arizona, or from Missouri and Kansas, through Colorado. All the anguish, the loneliness, the dry-blazing days and chill nights sprawled out across the continent. Came here, from New England in the 1840s, from Tennessee and Alabama in the late 1860s, from Oklahoma and Nebraska in the 1930s. The weather was never extreme. The people smiled. The vegetation was never wild, not like the kudzu and wisteria in Louisiana that grew everywhere, on houses, fences, weighing down young trees and clogging storm drains. Lance Boudreaux had left the Island and had found his way here, where the sun was pale, and the breeze cold and damp from the Pacific. Let him stay here and freeze, Mr. Landry thought. I should go home. Maybe he belongs here now. Maybe this is his country.

— Christ, Fourier said. Mr. Landry looked up to see a long-haired girl, slim and lovely, walking across the terrace, a big German shepherd on a leash behind her. She was naked above the waist except for an unbuttoned leather vest. She paused, looked around, and saw Fourier and Mr.

Landry staring at her. She walked over to the table and smiled. — Are you the lawyers looking for Lance?

Mr. Landry stood up, almost bowing. — Boudreaux. . . ?

— Ummm. Somebody said . . . you've got something for him.

— We represent the estate of his grandfather who . . .

— . . . kicked. . . ?

— Ummm. Yes. Gone now. Leaving only . . .

— Lance. How much?

Fourier grinned at her. — Don't ask, honey. You wouldn't believe it.

Mr. Landry frowned. — A substantial sum, he said. — Do you know. . . ?

— Ummm. Might. But I don't know you.

— What's the difference, Fourier asked.

— Narrow-minded people, the girl said. Her smile was lovely. She had a flower over her ear, tucked in her pale hair. — There are people, you know, *people* who don't like Lance. Who want to hurt us . . . him.

— We have certain papers, Mr. Landry began again. — Authentic acts . . .

— Wow, the girl said, leaning forward, shoulders back. Time stopped for Mr. Landry. Her breasts opened that same cool garden in his heart. Twilight came, and he felt a catch in his throat. He had not seen such things in so long.

— Wow, authentic . . . that's what Lance just loves. . . . He says you've got to feel it and then *do* it . . .

— Do what, Fourier asked, his eyes fixed not on hers, but down below.

— Anything, she said. — Any old thing at all. I'm Miz Minerva. You can call me Min . . .

— Can you take us. . . ? Mr. Landry asked, coming back from another place.

— Ummm. Gimme your name, and I'll let you know. I

got to tell Lance who it is . . . does he know you? I mean, really *know* you?

— No, Mr. Landry said. — No, I don't think so. But I knew his father and his mother. I knew his grandfather.

— Gee, Min said. — I never knew my father. I don't know if I even *had* a grandfather.

— Everybody has a grandfather, Fourier told her.

— Not *authentically*, Min said. — Not so they notice it. I don't even know where my father came from. I mean, he could have been from *Tanzania* . . .

— I doubt it, Fourier said dryly, moving his chair closer to Min's, his eyes scuttling about her like small animals.

— Christ, I don't even know anybody who ever *knew* their grandfather. In California . . . I mean, *nobody* in California . . .

— Yes, Mr. Landry said gently, — California . . .

— Okay, listen, Min said, seeming to lose interest in the talk. — I got to go now. I'll get back to you, huh?

— The Carleton Hotel, Fourier said. — You know?

— Oh yeah. See you . . .

She rose, one last movement of her shoulders leaving silence in her wake. Mr. Landry and Fourier stared at her as she left, the shepherd padding behind her. Mr. Landry finished his coffee. Fourier forgot his.

Min turned as she reached the broad walk that led to Telegraph Avenue. — See you . . .

VIII

They waited for two days, going no farther from the hotel than it took to eat, and even then leaving word and money with the clerk to pay street people to find them if a call should come from Min.

On the third evening, they were eating at Robbie's. A dollar and a quarter for all the chop suey and fried rice you could eat. Cafeteria style. Mr. Landry used his silverware.

Fourier had managed to learn his chopsticks in the time he had been there. Someone on the street was singing "Roll Over, Beethoven" at the top of his lungs. A police car passed, lights blinking, but no siren. Silent running. Fourier looked up. Satan's messenger was there. He held his tophat in his hand, turning the rim rapidly in his dirt-encrusted hands. He stared down at Mr. Landry, who paid him no mind, eating his chop suey slowly, turning the bean sprouts around the fork, as if it were spaghetti. His eyes were light, a peculiar green, and he paid no mind to Fourier.

— You are the one, he said portentously, flicking his cloak about him. — You are the *one* . . .

Mr. Landry looked up from his meal. — I doubt it, he said. — Get thee behind me, beast. And let him who saved the world send thee down to darkness . . . forever . . .

The Satanist backed away. — Forever . . . ?

Mr. Landry gave him a wintry smile. — For as long as there is . . .

— He sent me for you. He says you're supposed to come with me.

— Shit, Fourier blurted out. — Who sent you?

— The One Who Stands. He says for you to come . . .

Fourier looked at Mr. Landry. — I think I ought to whip up on this bastard, he said. Mr. Landry shook his head.

— You mean Lance Boudreaux, he asked.

— That is one of his manifestations, the Satanist said. — Now is the time. He could pass on at any moment.

— Oh, bullshit, Fourier said, pushing his chair back, his brow furrowed. Mr. Landry saw him for the first time as a country man, unhappy in the presence of evil, dejected in the presence of sin. Beyond his education, Fourier hated baseness for its own sake, and for the first time, Mr. Landry was reconciled to him. He reached out and touched Fourier's arm. — Louis, let it alone. We have to finish this.

They started to rise together, Fourier's eyes wide, having

heard for the first time his own Christian name in Mr. Landry's mouth. — Sure, yes sir. Right.

In the street, there was a Volkswagen van parked. It was covered with symbols: pentagrams, peculiar Latin quotations, a dragon with its tail in its mouth, an incredible creature possessing sexual organs both male and female, signs of the zodiac, the names of forgotten gods, Babylonian, Sumerian, Egyptian, and across the front, something with wings, terrible claws, and a great gaping scarlet emptiness where otherwise a face might be. Fourier looked at Mr. Landry as the side door slid open. Mr. Landry was about to nod when a boy dressed in work clothes with a necklace of seashells and a gold stud through his nostril twitched his sleeve. — From the hotel, he said, and Mr. Landry, forgetting he had left money with the clerk, handed him two dollars as he passed the paper over. On it was written in a small neat hand the words, "Raphael has something you need to know."

— The perfect master is waiting, the Satanist said.

— Hey, Fourier asked him, — you reckon Minerva is gonna be . . . wherever it is we're going?

— She is Helena, the Satanist whispered, — the great mother. She follows the Lance . . .

— She is one great mother, Fourier said. Then he looked at Mr. Landry. — A message from Min?

— No, Mr. Landry said, thinking whether to take time for a call or wait until later, until he had seen Lance Boudreaux III and gotten his business done.

— The time is now, the Satanist rasped, prodding Mr. Landry in the ribs. — Will you, won't you, will you, won't you, won't you . . .

Mr. Landry followed Fourier into the van. As the Satanist reached out to slide the door shut, Mr. Landry stared out into the darkness at him. — I won't, he said. — And when

this business is properly done, I mean to whip your
evil ass . . .

As the door slid shut, the last two things Mr. Landry
noticed were the leer of the Adversary, and the look of utter
astonishment on the face of young Fourier.

IX

It was somewhere in the mountains behind the university
near Strawberry Canyon as far as they could tell. The inside
of the van was even more bizarre than the outside. In there,
painted in some luminiscent pigment on plastic was a three-
panel mural of a Black Mass. The scene was set in the dark
center of a forest, like the Schwartzwald or the Ardennes.
There was a crescent moon standing high above the trees,
luminous clouds bathed in moon rays giving the appearance
of motion. Down below, in a clearing, and among the
gnarled leafless trees, figures of strange shapes moved toward
a central place where there stood a circle of stone, and in
its midst, an altar upon which lay a beautiful blond woman
who looked astonishingly like Minerva, her body nude,
full breasts pointed toward the dark skies, her eyes open,
fearless, staring upward at a presence poised above, body
formless as shadow and the lurid bearded face of a man. The
thing poised there held in a claw a piece of flint or granite
aimed not at her heart, but at her belly, full, as if with child.
There was an understanding between them, the demon
above, the demon below. Mr. Landry saw Fourier shiver,
his mouth twisted in disgust. Fourier had come to California
curious. He was beyond that now.

They drove. The van turned this way and that, moved
up into the hills past silent houses dark in the night. As they
rose higher, the fog began, that same fog that Mr. Landry
had seen before, coming in from the Pacific slowly in the
late afternoon before the sun faded behind it, inundating the

Golden Gate bridge, filling the bay. It seemed to cloak the van now, to swathe it and remove it from the town below or the mountains around. The Satanist sat in the front passenger seat. The driver beside him was hairless, his head and neck thick and bare. As he drove, Mr. Landry heard him breathe. It sounded as if he were snorting, as if he were angry or disgusted. He shifted gears violently, making the van jump as it slewed around the tight curves. The Satanist's hair was matted, as it lay in long greasy coils in the thread-bare, filthy collar of his cloak. Mr. Landry noticed that his own jaw was tight, so tight that he could not swallow. He had never been so close, staring ahead at someone he wanted to kill. It had grown on him slowly. At the campus, watching the dark cloak whirl, at the Chinese cafeteria, staring, claiming. To be a lawyer was to know that evil comes no harder than words or a turning away. The Satanist was a comic figure—no, rather he would be in the South. In Breauxville or New Orleans, his garb, his words would draw a crowd of puzzled yokels, black and white, perhaps a Baptist or a Witness who would frown and listen, and after a few amazed moments, swing, lash out and knock him down in front of the loungers and weekend shoppers while the laughter welled up all around. But here, somehow he had become real. As if the worship of death, sickness, disease of the soul, the Great Refusal, was the other face of a coin that stood on edge across the continent, Januslike, transposing realities. What was real in the South was fantasy here; what was real in California was a joke down South. To cross a desert is to pass through a door. Mr. Landry closed his eyes. He was there again, and his jaw lost its tension. The music was a fantasy, he thought. How right. He could not tell whether he was thinking or remembering. Something of Telemann. Quick, mercurial, terse. He felt a trace of cool wind across his face.

— Time to go in, he said aloud.

— What, Fourier said, a little too loudly, his voice piercing in the confines of the van. The Satanist twisted his head around. The driver snorted.

— Nothing, Mr. Landry said quickly, realizing that the breeze he had felt was not off the Mississippi or Lake Pontchartrain. The Satanist had opened his window and was lighting a thick cigarette wrapped in brown paper.

— You all right, Fourier asked Mr. Landry in a whisper.
— Is it getting to you?

Mr. Landry smiled. — Fine, he said. One of the results of aging in the law is that you are not easily gotten to. By the time you have been at it thirty or forty years, you have done so many things no one should have to do that something has drained out of you, to be replaced with the law, like a creature trapped in mud which is hard pressed for a long, long time, leaching away the soft parts, making everything over. In stone.

He remembered going to Houston to identify that woman who had been Lance Boudreaux III's mother. She lay nude on a chrome shelf that slid out of a wall. He did not recognize her face. It was distant, cool, wholly at peace. He had never known her that way. It was the wedding ring, bitten deep into the flesh of her finger, that he knew. He remembered wondering why she had not had it cut off, sold it or thrown it away. What had she loved, what hated? He took her back to be buried on the Island. The Old Man had little ceremony. One evening the coffin arrived, the next morning it was buried next to the gravestone with Lance Boudreaux II carved upon it, underneath which there was nothing. Because nothing had been sent home. Because there had been nothing to send.

That had not mattered to the Old Man. Because almost nothing mattered to him. Except that he had a fine sense of symmetry, and there in less than an acre were all those who had gone before, or at least a stone to note their having been. And a stone for a dead son disintegrated over Roumania. And the body of a woman who would rather have been dumped in the landfill of East New Orleans than be laid to eternal rest in that soil just offshore, under the eyes of that old man.

— Where, Mr. Landry had asked, — is Lance.

— In school, the old man had said, drawing his pipe, striking it on a stone named for some anonymous Didier who had died in this place, whose relation to it was not even known to those whose forebears had lived here a hundred years. — Nothing. No need . . .

Mr. Landry frowned, trying to remember what his fee had been for bringing her home. It had been high. He charged the Old Man not simply on the difficulty or importance of the matter, but on whether he wanted to do it or not. He had not wanted to. Had not wanted to look upon her dead face, nor see to it that she was brought in death to the place she had fled in life. Not because he honored her unspoken wish, or even felt he should. She was Lance II's chief mistake, compared to which crashing his fighter was no more than a minor slip. But it seemed cowardly to bring one dead to a place she would not have willingly come to in life. It had not been the first time he had done such a thing—indisputably from cowardice that other time—and so he charged a great deal for his bad conscience. It had not helped at all.

The van skidded to a stop, the motor died, and in the silence following, all he could hear was the snorting of the bald driver whose face he had not even seen. No one moved for a long moment. Outside, the fog was so thick that Mr. Landry could see nothing. There was only the weird glow from the black lights which illuminated the murals. Then, almost without motion, the Satanist opened the door and stepped outside. He disappeared into the fog, but they could hear him breaking underbrush, crushing leaves, then his footsteps sounded crisply, as if on brick or flagstone.

— Come on, he called from the fog. — Come on.

Fourier reached over and opened the sliding door of the van. Tendrils of fog and the chill night air invaded, making the inside like the outside, the outside like the inside. Mr. Landry stepped out gingerly and waited for Fourier whose arm he took. Not because Fourier could see any better than he, but because Fourier could stand a broken leg better. Young legs mend. They should shoot old men with broken legs. They mended no better than horses.

— Why won't you come on, the Satanist's voice came from the darkness. — He waits.

Fourier cursed under his breath. — He can goddamn well wait.

Mr. Landry clucked at him. — You sound like you belong here.

He could hear Fourier's breath catch. — No sir, no way. These are not my people.

They turned a corner or topped a hill. Even later, trying to reconstruct that moment, they could remember only that one moment they were in darkness, the next in light. There were eucalyptus trees and Pacific cypress all around, a fountain in the center of a Spanish patio illuminated softly by hidden lights. To their left there was a glass table, beyond French doors soft light, and piano music from within.

It was Mr. Landry's turn to gasp. He almost staggered, reached out to steady himself against a tree trunk. He closed his eyes and listened. The second French suite. She had played it when she was very happy, very sure of herself. The stone in him began to melt. There were still soft parts. He began to move toward the open French doors. The fog was thicker now, and he felt its moisture condensing on his face.

— Whoa, Fourier said, catching his arm. — Wait for me.

As they reached the door, the music stopped, and he

could hear the rustle of pages turning. He stepped through the door and brought himself to look to the left, where the piano was, where it should be. There was nothing but a large chair, an ottoman, and a low table where a pipe smoked in a marble ashtray. He turned back, confused. Across the room, there was music again. Something from Haydn, a sonata.

— Hi, Minerva said, her fingers moving quickly across the keyboard. She wore a long sari of some peculiar shade between blue and green.

— Uh, hi, Fourier began, but the volume of the music suddenly rose, and its character changed. It was the "March of the Meistersinger." Fourier turned, and across the room, he saw Lance Boudreaux III.

Mr. Landry shook his head to rid it of the pain of remembering. The man coming into the room had long hair, a beard, and a long sarape. He was tall, broad, his belly beginning to sag. There was a long scar that began on his temple and vanished into the beard. He was smiling, and he swept across the bare wooden floor toward Fourier. — The lawyer, he said. — You're the lawyer from down there.

His voice was low and smooth, and it filled the room, covering the piano's last notes, the snuffling of the driver who stood now at the French doors with the Satanist. Mr. Landry saw his face for the first time. It was sallow and wrinkled. The driver looked as old as Mr. Landry at first glance. His eyes were round and large and deep. His nose was like a beak. He and the Satanist seemed to be waiting for something.

Fourier's eyes were almost as wide as the driver's.
— That's him, over there, he managed to get out, pointing at Mr. Landry. Lance turned slowly, and Mr. Landry could see him in three-quarter and profile before they stood face to face. He tried to see in any view some semblance, some

resonance from the past that would recall the room in the old house on the Island, and the small hunched figure leaning, chin in hands, over a large shabby book. There was nothing. Not a hint.

— Uncle René, Lance Boudreaux said. His smile was a light source. — You came all the way here . . . to see me. All the way out . . . here.

— Lance, Mr. Landry answered, automatically extending his hand.

Lance Boudreaux took it in both of his. His fleshy face, handsome, deepset dark eyes, was aglow with unfeigned pleasure. — So long, Lance said. — What? Almost fifteen years now.

— Nearer twenty.

Lance Boudreaux's smile broadened. He took Mr. Landry's arm and steered him toward a rough Mexican-style staircase. — No, he said softly, as they began to climb the stairs. — That last time . . . you didn't see me . . . behind the house, in the graveyard.

Mr. Landry found himself breathing heavily as they reached the landing. From down below, he could hear Minerva's playing. Something dark, dominant. A Rachmaninov prelude, he thought. — That day . . . the cemetery . . . but your grandfather said . . . you were in school.

They climbed higher, past the second floor, into a small room with heavily timbered, time-darkened stucco walls, but with large high windows that opened the walls to the night. Down below, the lights of the bay area curved like a necklace from Richmond down to San José, with San Francisco a shining pendant obscured and concealed by waves of fog. They paused there silently watching the festival of lights.

Lance Boudreaux poured brandy into two large snifters. He and Mr. Landry drank. Then he poured again.

— No. In the magnolia, the great big one. Not thirty feet away. I could hear . . . Lance Boudreaux fell silent, his eyes clouding. — Nothing. No need. He didn't even want me to see her then.

Mr. Landry threw down his brandy and poured another. The music from below, like the distant lights, was faint, shuddering over the distance from its source. This place, the very state itself, was cold as a tomb when darkness came. Brandy was what was wanted.

— But I did . . .

— Did what. . . ?

— I saw her. When youall were gone. When it was dark. Then she was mine. I had my tools, the archaeological tools. The ones he bought me when I said I wanted to go with her and he said, no, you can't do that, but you can go anywhere else, and I said all right, the Yucatan, thinking that will do it, he'll let me go with her, and if I do, she'll come to love me. But he sent me down there. Honest to God. Bought all the stuff, hired guides, a campsite, maps from the Center for Mesoamerican Studies. That was when I realized that you could do anything, or even stop anything, if you had the money and laid it on the barrelhead. You remember Hamilton, the big nigger? The one who ran the sheds and killed that little Frenchman Espagnol who tried to burn the place when he was fired? Sure, you remember. You defended him. You got him off. He took me down there, Hamilton did. We went down and dug and dug. For months. Snakes, spiders the size of your hand, tropical storms. Your skin got to mildewing. But we got down . . . Mixtec, Olmec . . . I have pieces in the National Museum. Where the screen of water falls in the courtyard . . .

Lance turned away, still talking. In the semidarkness, lit only by an enormous menorah, tapers almost as large as paschal candles, each of a different height, Mr. Landry could hardly make him out, could see only his outline against the stars and lights. His voice was no longer the splendid captivating bass it had been below. It was soft, reedy, almost preadolescent, and the hurt in it was as palpable as the quick sear of the brandy as it speared the throat. There is a kind of speech that passes between men which seeks to tell, and another kind which aims only to evoke, to establish a thing in another mind free of judgment or consideration. Lance's speech was of that second kind. Mr. Landry was not a listener. He was a hearer now. He was a familiar singularity from the past, a point in the field of Lance Boudreaux's recollection, something like a milepost long passed, something to fix those old days amidst the flux of these.

— . . . when it was dark, I dug down with my tools. The dirt was soft. Down to my own beginning, to my denial. I opened the coffin, and she was still there. I didn't even recognize her. She was a stranger I might once have walked past in the French Quarter, a face I might have seen in a car passing along Highway 61. Sleeping in Christ, the priest had said just a few hours before. But empirical observation proved that false. She was dead in there. She'd never sleep again. The undertaker's paste was shrinking, and I could see where . . . the fall. She had fallen a very long way . . .

Mr. Landry stared at Lance's back as he reached for the bottle. He was beginning to listen now. — My God, why . . . ?

Lance turned back, but he was paying Mr. Landry no mind even as he took the bottle from Mr. Landry's hand and poured the large snifter full again. He was not telling Mr. Landry anything. He was living it again. Mr. Landry happened to be present. That was good, because it would not do for just anyone to be present. No, not quite that. More than present: a cause, a reason for the reliving, though not an efficient cause, not a sufficient reason.

— Looking very prim. Like she'd never taken a drink,

never hired her a dago lover, never done a wrong thing. Like being dead was a cure and answer to everything, like it made everything all right . . .

Mr. Landry poured the last of the brandy into his glass. Even before he could raise it to his lips, Lance Boudreaux drew out another from some hidden trove, breached it, and filled his own glass again, then topped up Mr. Landry's. On the Island, in the Mansion, Mr. Landry suddenly remembered, that had been all the hard liquor there was. No bourbon, no scotch, no gin. Courvoisier V.S.O.P., or one had to dip into a bewildering array of vintage wines from France, some dating back to the 1880s. I think I'm getting to be an alcoholic, Mr. Landry thought. I forgot how much I could handle . . . even after she . . . I held together. But this one trip. In the long run, he tried to remember what Keynes had said. In the long run, we succeed . . . at nothing.

— . . . said goodbye. Not to her. The hell with her. I just had to see the actual physical source for what I was saying good-bye to. It was the loneliness, the waiting for her at least to come see me between studs, even if she couldn't do her plain duty, what even a lousy white-trash family like hers must have raised her to do, or there wouldn't have been any children from them . . .

The brandy had reached Mr. Landry by then. He was distanced from what he saw and heard. The room took on the character of a stage turning slowly above the distant city lights, the faded music below, the wheeling stars.

— . . . then I poured in the kerosene and set it off . . .

Mr. Landry heard him, but it didn't matter. He was noticing how the stars looked like reflections of the lights of San Francisco in a profound and darkened pool.

— . . . nothing but carbon. How could carbon, a little calcium, and some trace elements have hurt me so much? That's when I decided to do physics, to do religions, too. Medicine wasn't going to be enough. Later, years later, each time I practiced medicine, I thought, this is only carbon, some mess of elements you're patching or adjusting. It will fall again. There's no truth here. Not at this magnitude . . .

Mr. Landry heard, but he was not listening. He lifted his full glass in a silent toast to the half circle of lights down there, to the strains of a muffled Scarlatti sonata which shivered on the crisp California air. The brandy, the music, and the stars were real. The rest was a delusion. Old men suffer those when they have been alone a very long time.

— . . . then I put her back. I was done with her. Like those three dago chauffeurs who walked away when they had got whatever it was they wanted from her. More than that. I pushed the archaeological tools in, too. Because I was done with digging, rooting in the earth, the past. Once, when I was small, I had thought to go to Roumania, to pay whatever they'd charge to let me dig until I found him . . . So I could look, even if at nothing more than broken bones and bits of khaki cloth. If only that, then that at least. She cured me that night, translated me to physics, to magic . . .

Squinting, Mr. Landry had noticed movement in the grove of trees below, out behind the main house. A man, tiny as an ant, with long hair, came to the side of a large swimming pool. He led a child by the hand. He began to bathe the child in the water. A thin cloud of vapor rose from the pool. Beyond the pool, Mr. Landry saw others. A fire or two outside small tents or shacks apparently thrown together out of plywood and tar paper. The more closely he focused his eyes, the more he could see.

Mr. Landry pointed down there. — What. . . ?

— Niggers, Lance Boudreau said quickly. — They're my niggers.

Mr. Landry shook his head. The man and child at the pool were, even at this distance, obviously not black.

— But . . .

— No, they're niggers. I scooped 'em up and brought 'em

here. Off the roads, out of the alleys. Got some of 'em at the hospital while I worked there. Fair number from jail. Listen, I got a Louisiana state trooper down there youall sent out to find me. But it don't matter. What you got is just pieces of people. Hands, hearts, brains, guts, all the other things. But not a goddamned one with all of it together. They see me saving 'em. If I say, work, and bring it all back home to me, they do it.

He smiled crookedly. — Now, if I was to say, go kill, 'cause that's what has to be ... why, they would. Look at 'em down there. They live like niggers, they think like niggers. They're my people. They need me ... and they go out and dance and shuffle and beg in the streets and bring me whatever they get. Nothing held back. I make a nice crop ...

Mr. Landry sat down. Lance Boudreaux opened one of the large windows and stepped out onto a balcony beyond.

— See, Uncle René, these people are fellahin. Racked up, burned out. They were clerks or waitresses. They managed filling stations or ran a minigolf. One of 'em was a computer programmer. Some of 'em were at the university. There's a few come back from Viet Nam with their heads on upside down. Lots of musicians and artists. Writers. I think there's even a lawyer out there. Couple of doctors. One did five big ones for controlled substances. The other one got ruined with a malpractice suit. Wouldn't let him operate on a dead goat. But they're all laid back now. They hang around and take groceries from me and smoke grass I pick up across the bay. Nobody asks 'em anything. Nobody breaks their hearts. They do what I say, and the rest is okay ...

—The one downstairs ... they're insane. The one in the dirty cloak thinks you're God ... or ...

— Satanas. Yeah, well, they're probably right. What the hell ... they never came across anything like me before ...

Lance Boudreaux turned around unsteadily. He had put

aside the snifter and was drinking from the bottle now. His grin was visible through the mass of beard. — Hell, you've seen 'em in the streets. Any son of a bitch who can drink a quart of whiskey and still walk, anybody who can make a decision and stick to it. Anybody who can handle that little madonna downstairs—that's a god. Or a devil. They're wreckage, Uncle René, zombies. To a zombie, a living man's a god. To a woman surrouded by freaks, a man who stands is a god. Don't you take it too serious. People always construct what they need. It don't have anything to do with you or the people back home. Anyhow, everything is full of gods, remember?

Mr. Landry shook his head. He did not remember. Everything is full of pain. Whatever you love is certain to die. Nothing gets better with age. What does it mean for a man to claim he is a god? Is it a way of saying he can't be hurt any more?

— It's just the Island again, Lance Boudreaux said abstractedly. — Only bigger. The old man would love it. He could have taken over California. Nobody leaves me. I'm . . . their life. That's what he had, isn't it? He didn't just live his own life. He lived the Island and every son of a bitch on it. Now he's dead, and you come for me. He had everything but *droit du seigneur*, and if he'd wanted those hairy-legged slatterns, he'd of had that too.

Mr. Landry found that he had carried his thin briefcase up the stairs with him. He put it down on a dark slate table covered with cunningly wrought symbols, and fanned out a large bundle of legal-sized sheets.

— I have the papers, he said, as if he had heard nothing that had gone before. — You must accept the succession. No need for benefit of inventory . . . there were no debts to speak of . . .

Lance Boudreaux paid no mind. He went on drinking, talking, staring alternately up at the stars and down at the lights. He paid no mind to the man and child beside the pool who had somehow heard his distant voice and now knelt side by side, arms extended upward toward him. Others around the fires and in the tents and shacks had heard, too, and slowly came through the fog to gather around the pool.

— It bothers you, Uncle René, those . . . things I got down there . . .

Mr. Landry paused. In court or out, he always paused when what he would say had not been long considered. Words have consequences.

— Lancelot, he said at last, and softly, — I am very old and tired, too. This trip, this place—I mean the state—these people cause me great discomfort. I only want to do my duty and go home . . .

— Ah, Lance Boudreaux said as softly. He came back into the room and squatted beside Mr. Landry. — Duty . . . the most sublime word in the English language . . .

Mr. Landry looked at him in astonishment, but Lance Boudreaux's expression behind the dense beard bore no sign, not the slightest, of irony or sardonic intention.

— Look out there, Uncle René . . . see 'em coming? They want a look at me. See? It's my duty . . . they want to see their god . . .

Lance stood up, swayed a moment, belched, and stepped back onto the balcony, falling against the rail, recovering. A chill shard of breeze carried back to Mr. Landry the smell of brandy and a strange carnal odor, that which one comes upon in a zoo. By the wolves, by the great cats.

He threw up his arms as if to bless them, and the nearly empty bottle of brandy looped upward from his hand and then spiraled down to fall into the pool, troubling the motionless waters. Immediately those below began jumping into the pool to recover the mystery vouchsafed them.

— See, Lance Boudreaux said, his voice beginning to blur.

— Even if they're wrong, they won't be the first . . . Baal, Astarte, Mazda . . . we bring the poor bastards comfort. Just by standing. Look at 'em . . .

Mr. Landry arose only a little steadier than Lance. He stepped carefully to the opening where he could see. Down there, the tiny people, garbed in rags and outrageous costumes, were drinking from the bottle, passing it from hand to hand, touching their naked children with the liquor. From behind and below, he could hear the unutterably distant sound of the piano: "pavane pour une infante defunte," slow, solemn, each note a threnody.

Lance Boudreaux turned, leaned precariously against the rail now, outlined by stars above, lights below. — He . . . left it all . . . to me. . . ?

Mr. Landry was still looking down at the pool. It made him sad. Nothing changes. Only appearances. The beast remains what he always was. — What? Yes. There was no one else . . . yes. All of it. Some was always yours under Louisiana law. By representation . . .

— . . . ?

— . . . your father's legitime . . . his forced portion . . .

— My father? But he . . .

— It doesn't matter. Our law chains the generations together. Through property if nothing else . . . if you should have a child . . .

— Ah, Lance Boudreaux muttered, coming inside, almost slamming the door. — You see, they worship wholeness . . . the deaf sob for music, the blind for color and form, the soulless for a movement within that tells them they're alive, tells them what to do. The Island hurt me. But it took nothing away . . . you're a god, too . . .

Mr. Landry almost smiled. This time he paused only for an instant. — No. Not me . . .

— You're from down there, from home. You're still whole. You could . . .

Mr. Landry did smile, a wretched smile not fit to see.
— . . . Become vice-regent of California? No, only the young
are gods. And they get cured. One way or the other . . .

He quickly folded up the papers as Lance Boudreaux
found still another bottle of brandy. No one would be signing anything tonight. He could not imagine why he had
even taken the papers out. It was his opinion that Lancelot
Boudreaux III was not of sound mind. If he was to succeed
to his grandfather's estate without a curator, there would
be a hearing first. And in Louisiana, not here. God knows
not here. No place west of Texas. Perhaps no place west
of the Sabine River.

Lance Boudreaux did not notice Mr. Landry putting the
papers away. He was drinking, talking. Not to Mr. Landry.
Not even to himself.

— . . . take the sons of bitches to the Island. Solitude. Isola-
tion. Carbon and a little calcium . . . traces . . . it doesn't
matter so long as you don't let 'em hurt . . . don't let 'em
hope. No, hurt . . .

Mr. Landry began the long treacherous descent down the
unlighted stairs, tottering now and again, hearing the heavy
tread of Lance Boudreaux close behind him. It crossed his
mind to wonder if Lance was homicidal or simply dotty,
taken with the kind of mania, the mild will to one thing so
common along St. Charles Avenue and in the quiet old
uptown streets where familes had lived well over a century,
ruminating on the whirlwind which had enwrapped them
when Mr. Jefferson bought them from the bourgeois em-
peror of the French. Quietists who had never heard of Port
Royale; Jansenists who supposed they had invented self-
denial and punishment; exorcists who used Jack Daniels to
put away the business that stalks at noon; ancient feckless
magicians living on dividends who had been taking moderate
doses of cocaine since the time it was legally used as an
ingredient of Coca Cola.

They reached the bottom floor. Mr. Landry saw Fourier seated next to Minerva on the narrow piano bench. The top of her sari was loose and when she leaned forward over the keyboard, Fourier would lean with her. At the French doors, the Satanist and the driver had not moved. Their eyes caught Lance Boudreaux as if they expected instruction or revelation. Minerva was playing one of the Brahms piano sonatas now—no, it was the theme from the Second Piano Quartet.

Lance Boudreaux stumbled behind the long ornate bar. Back there, it was dark mirrored panels. The bar top was of black marble with chrome accents. Art deco, they had called it, Mr. Landry remembered. It had gotten nowhere in New Orleans. Only the WPA had made use of it here and there in parks and public buildings. It belonged in California.

— . . . forced portion, Lance muttered to himself. — I get that. No matter what. From my father. Listen, he said louder, so that the Satanist and the driver could hear. So that Minerva, Fourier, and Mr. Landry could hear him.

— Listen, down South, where the old gods were, where the new gods will arise, they have these laws. Families are big. This is my Uncle René, because when I was too small even to know what an uncle was, that's what they told me to say. And it's real, because he never went away. He is an old bastard who brings the law down, who hasn't got the smoke of life left in him, but he was always there. Like the goddamned statue of the Confederate dead. He never bought a trailer and moved away or had a divorce . . . and now he's brought me . . .

Lance fell forward against the polished black marble bar. — He's brought me to my . . . kingdom . . .

Mr. Landry felt his face turn red. But why should it? This was no court. It was not even Louisiana, and as for whatever it might be that Lance Boudreaux called the smoke of life, he was most surely right. It had drifted away one morning light-years ago on a silent patio in a town across the universe. When the music stopped.

— You can't keep things . . . from the kids, Lance Boudreaux gasped, laughing into his water tumbler of brandy.

The Satanist and the driver stared at Lance Boudreaux. Then they stared at Mr. Landry. Then they began to snicker. Quietly at first, then more loudly. The eyes of the driver were wide, insane. He had come close to Mr. Landry now, and there was a rank, sickening stench about him. He was not an old man as he appeared from a distance. He was quite young. But his skin was incredibly wrinkled, his features pinched as if his face had been squeezed in a vise.

As they laughed, Lance Boudreaux rose up from his elbows behind the bar. He paused there as if posed against the back bar for photographs to be taken, a wide smile spreading across his bearded face. He nodded his head toward the mirrored shelves behind, raised his eyebrows. The Satanist pointed gleefully, the driver slapped him on the back. Mr. Landry followed their eyes, past the bar, past Lance Boudreaux III, to a shelf of the back bar where, amidst bottles of gin and crème de menthe, was a jar containing a thing something like a pig, curled members inward, and which, heedless of gravity, hovered like a tiny dancer, its something like a mouth caught in a permanent leer, unfinished limbs swaying amidst the cloudy fluid, filled with a faint golden dust composed it seemed of cells of the thing itself. And at the base of the jar there was an irregularly trimmed paper tab posted upon which was written in a neat hand, LANCE ST. C. BOUDREAUX IV.

It was then, just as Mr. Landry's eyes registered the jar, its contents, and its label, that the flat distant emotionless voice seemed to sound within the room itself.

— This is the police. You in the house. Throw down your

arms. Come out with your hands on your heads. This is
the police. You in the house . . .

Throw down your arms, Mr. Landry frowned. What is
that supposed to mean? Then he saw the guns . . .

The driver and the Satanist had M-16s. They had gotten
them from behind the bar and were moving toward the
French doors. Lance Boudreaux came up from behind the
bar with something that looked like a sten gun, except
that it had a large round barrel, and an enormous clip below. — This is the appointed time, dogs, Lance Boudreaux
shouted. — The beast is here . . .

Mr. Landry looked across the room. Minerva was standing beside the piano with a Kalasnikov assault rifle.
Fourier was moving back from the piano as Minerva turned
to a window, broke it with the barrel of her gun, and fired
a burst out across the patio, into the fog. But before the
echoes of her fire had died away, the room was annihilated.
Mr. Landry dropped from his barstool to the floor. Falling,
he heard and saw the striated mirrors behind the bar shatter, the shards of glass flying like shot across the room, as
the lamp near the piano exploded into pieces. He could
not see Fourier, but even in the darkness he could hear him.
— Son of a bitch, gimme a goddamned gun . . .

— No, Mr. Landry called out. — Let it be, Fourier . . .
let it be.

Everything was fine down there for Mr. Landry. The
clatter of gunfire did not disturb him. He had closed his
eyes, thinking this was God's will, he would go on here in
California. Why not? Why shouldn't a man die in a foreign
place? He was surely justified, being in this artificial hell
by way of doing his duty, wasn't he? Afterward, someone
would surely send him home.

Above, he heard that rich deep voice so alien that he
felt even now he should recognize it. — I am the one who

stands . . . they cannot end this thing we have begun . . .

But by then the fire from outside had become incredible. It was as if some one out there were throwing masses of metal into the room. Bullets hit the piano, and Mr. Landry could hear the strange harmony of strings plucked randomly. Another burst raked the bar just above his head, and he heard bottles and glasses breaking. It crossed his mind to wonder if, among the bottles of bourbon, scotch, and gin, that jar had been shattered, its contents poured out on the shelves of the back bar.

At the French doors, he could see the driver and the Satanist. The Satanist was standing, firing at random into the fog. The driver knelt, firing too. Suddenly, there was light, and following it, another shattering blast of fire. Mr. Landry saw the Satanist fall, a mist of blood and flesh spraying from him. The cloak flew up, and Mr. Landry could see the dirty starched shirt shatter, pieces of it flying away as the Satanist stumbled backward, his voice suddenly louder than the gunshots. — Diabolus . . . Dominus . . . Then it was quiet again, and the Satanist lay sprawled backward, part of his head gone, his body riddled. Thank God, Mr. Landry thought. So far, so good.

— Fourier, Mr. Landry called out.

— Sir, Mr. Landry heard from across the room.

— Stay down, you hear?

— Yes sir, I do. But Minerva . . .

— Hit her one up side her head, Fourier. That's best . . .

— Yes sir . . .

Then there was another burst of fire, and in the midst of it, Mr. Landry saw shadows out on the patio. The driver rose up from the floor, and as he did, there was a brilliant interlock of lights from outside. They fell across the driver, and at that moment there was a stab of flame from outside which quenched itself in the body of the driver who, in the very instant of dying, shouted, O Unknown Lord . . .

As some of the shadows from the patio entered the room, materializing into men in black uniforms with what looked to Mr. Landry like baseball caps, and dark short guns, there was suddenly a strange whispering sound from just above, from behind the bar. The figures coming through the French doors spun backward, one falling into the piano, another into an end table, spilling a lamp and ashtrays across the floor. Mr. Landry craned his neck and saw Lance Boudreaux III leaning forward over the bar, a long thick-barreled gun pointing out toward the darkness.

— Who's next, he roared in a harsh country accent.
— Come on, boys. My ass is a cabbage patch. There's enough here for all you sons of bitches . . .

Later Mr. Landry would remember his own astonishment, thinking of that language, those words, welling up amidst death and disorder, in the wake of death befuddled by mystery. He never left home, Mr. Landry remembered thinking. Never even left.

Then he looked up, and once more the shadows were invading, only this time their guns were firing. As they moved across the room, Mr. Landry saw a blur behind the piano. For a fraction of a second, he thought it was Fourier, and he almost rose himself to shout him down, out of the path of what he knew would be coming even before he could shout. But it wasn't Fourier, and as he focused on the girl, Minerva rose from behind the piano, her sari pulled down, her long blond hair hanging down, veiling her golden breasts.

— Hey, she cried at the shadows, — hey . . .

For the smallest of instants, the shadows turned, they and their weapons tranced, as if they were substantial, of flesh instead of mist. Then, as Mr. Landry watched in horror, Minerva raised from the shattered keyboard of the piano the assault rifle, aiming it at the shadows. But there were others coming from behind who had seen nothing but the

motion itself, as if it were disembodied. The bullets stitched across her breasts, planting ghastly scarlet flowers there, slapping her backward like the blow of a callous lover.
— Oh wow, she whispered from the darkness down there.

The shadows turned then, and Mr. Landry thought they were about to fire at him. They strode into the light and he could see that they were men, young men, whose faces were darkened with burnt cork. Their guns were not pointing at him, though, and he saws their eyes shining out above their smudged cheeks, aimed behind the bar . . .

— Praise the Lord, Mr. Landry heard Lance Boudreaux yell. — you godless scumbags . . .

He heard that peculiar whispering sound again, and then the deafening clatter of the guns before him. One of the shadows fell, his baseball cap coming off, showing his light hair, his white forehead, clearly dead. Behind the bar, something was struggling, thrashing in the broken glass back there, snuffling, sounding like some kind of animal. — Ah, ah, ah, it croaked. I am ready, Mr. Landry thought. Lord God, I am surely ready now. But the sounds went on, and after another moment, there were arms lifting Mr. Landry from the floor, assisting him across the rubble scattered over the floor, past the bleeding bodies of the Satanist and the driver. The last thing he could remember later concerning that night was Fourier, dirty, confused, covered with blood not his own, half stumbling, half supported by a pair of shadows like those who were carrying Mr. Landry. Somehow, they were brought close together, the two of them.

— Aw shit, René, aw Jesus, you know what's happened . . . young Fourier blurted.

For a small moment Mr. Landry didn't answer him. He was trying to gather himself back together. Fourier was an associate. It was important to give good example. Always. Even then.

— Yes, Mr. Landry managed to cough out. — I know. Everything. It . . . it's all right . . .

He lost consciousness then. He had never lied to an associate before.

X

Mr. Landry came to himself aboard Flight 671. He had recollections of what had passed in between. He remembered being carried out to an ambulance stretcher. He remembered Lieutenant Raphael poised there above him, his face red, suffused with anger.

— You crazy old bastard, Raphael was saying, — why didn't you . . . the boy said you got my note . . . the people in Daly City . . . it was Lance . . .

— Because, Mr. Landry remembered saying, — because it wasn't right . . .

— Right?

— Never mind, Mr. Landry remembered telling him.
— You couldn't understand. It's . . .

— Couldn't understand . . . what was . . . right . . . ?

Mr. Landry remembered feeling a certain triumph then, a certain fulfillment. —Right . . . not what was . . . right.

They were in the sky now, above Las Vegas according to the pilot. Heading back to New Orleans. At least that is what the pilot said, taking into account his accent, translating what the pilot was telling the passengers. Back to New Orleans.

Mr. Landry looked to his left. He was seated on the aisle. At the window was Fourier, his head bandaged, his eyes downcast. Mr. Landry studied him, considering what he had been to begin with, what he was now. He was pleased, Mr. Landry was. Not simply with this boy, this Louis Fourier, but with himself as well. The very essence of life, he considered, was to have something set before you, something that had to be done. And to achieve it, to do what needed to be done.

He shook his head slowly, trying to clear it of the shadows, the uncertainties. He was not quite right just yet. There were still blank spots in his memory—as there had been when he had been called upon to appear before the Superior Court in and for Marin County, the State of California.

He looked up, and the stewardess was before him. She was tall and tanned, her body luxurious, her smile certain and assured. She bent down over him. — I'm Kim, she said. — Is there anything I can get you . . . ?

Mr. Landry smiled up at her, his eyes meeting hers and holding them. — I would like a . . . double martini and some writing paper, he said softly.

Kim's eyes swept past him, holding for a moment on the unmoving figure between him and Fourier.

Then her eyes moved onward. — Excuse me, sir, she said to Fourier. — What would you like to drink?

Fourier made no response at first. He was staring out of the window, down into the Grand Canyon. Kim spoke again, and his eyes moved from the depths 35,000 feet below. — Honey, he said, — lemme have a double martini right now, and keep 'em coming every ten minutes till we get home . . . I mean New Orleans, you dig?

Kim stared at him, then at the bandaged burden between him and Mr. Landry. — Yes, of course, sir, she said, moving away a little faster than she might have, had it not been for the certain tension she felt there.

No one spoke for a long moment after she moved down the aisle. Mr. Landry heard the smooth insistent roar of the jet engines behind them.

—Lord God, Fourier breathed, — you know, I . . . I think I really . . . loved her . . .

For a long moment Mr. Landry said nothing. His eyes

were pressed shut. Yes, he knew that. Yes, he knew. That
for the rest of his life, Fourier would remember that.
— Louis, he said, — you got to get used to . . . losing. You
know what I mean.
— Yessir, young Fourier said. — I mean, I really do understand . . .
Mr. Landry saw Fourier's eyes fixed on the seat between
them. The seat where Lance Boudreaux III sat, his head
bandaged, his eyes fixed on the front of the first-class com-
partment, unmoving, steady as the rock and sand below
over which the plane was passing. The bandage on his head
was not as large as the one Fourier wore, and his close-
shaven face was free of emotion. He looked like a slightly
pudgy boy of twenty or so. Depending on how you looked,
and from what angle, there appeared to be a slight smile
on his lips.
The stewardess returned with the drinks and some paper.
— Thank you, Kim, Mr. Landry said, smiling up at her.
He took the paper she handed him, and as he sipped his
drink, took out a pen, and began to sketch out the terms of
an order of interdiction he would file with the court when
they reached home. Fourier watched him glumly. — They
should of killed the son of a bitch, he said softly, — instead
of giving him to you. I'd never of given him to you . . .
he'd never of gotten out of my jurisdiction alive . . .
Mr. Landry went on writing. — He's a dead man to the
law, he said slowly. — You heard the doctors. The bullets
blasted away everything. Everything. We're taking home a
carcass. There's nothing there . . . It eats and sleeps . . .
Fourier was silent for a moment. — . . . killed all them
people, he said. — . . . ought to push him out of this plane . . .
— Louis, Louis, Mr. Landry said, shaking his head, sipping
his drink.
It was then, as Fourier turned away and leaned his head
against the window, eyes closed, that Mr. Landry felt his

sleeve being twitched. He felt cold for a moment, but when he turned, it was only the clawed hand of Lance Boudreaux III aimlessly scratching. As Mr. Landry looked, Lance's face remained what it had been since that night when the police ambulance had come to take him away from the shambles of the house in the canyon, a sea of tranquility, depthless, imperturbable, purposeless. But as he reached over to free his sleeve, the hand plucked his pen away. Before he could even attempt to retrieve it, the hand, moving as if it had a life of its own, settled on the paper on Mr. Landry's tray. In large childish letters the hand quickly traced out something almost unintelligible, yet obviously more than random scrawl. Then the hand was done, the pen lying beside his martini glass.

Mr. Landry squinted to read. Yet . . . still. I am the . . . One Who. Stands.

Mr. Landry picked up the paper, stared at it, then crumpled it into a ball before he could bring himself to look at Lance Boudreaux.

When at last he did, nothing had changed. Except that the impression of a smile on Lance Boudreaux's lips was much stronger. A virtual certainty.

Mr. Landry threw down his martini and lay back in his seat. They were hardly half an hour into their trip, and they had still a long way to go.

A Day in Thy Court

For a day in thy court is better than a thousand.
Psalms 84:10

I

When the bass struck, it was like nothing else he had ever experienced. He could not count the fish he had caught in his life. But the way it happened with bass had never gotten old. Each time was a beginning. Even now, he could look forward to rising early, walking down to the old boat dock, moving almost soundlessly out across the mirror-smooth lake to the river. If there was a single thing he would re-member from this long dwindling botch men were pleased to call life, it would be this time, those times that were a single time as the Indians had known, a single fish, a single fisherman in the twilight beyond the death of the last day and before the rising of the next. He did not remember her. Nor did he remember not remembering.

He had lapped his fly line into a pocket of shadow so deep that he had only known the popper was placed because he heard it fall clean and saw the merest reflection of the ripples that fanned out from it. He had let it lie, then drawn back a foot or so of the line. It was as if someone had taken a motion picture of the small yellow fly lying twitching on the dark water until the bass hit, and then had edited it, cutting out those frames that showed the fish striking. So that there was only film before and after, but no picture at all of the instant when the fly vanished below the surface in a blur of foamy water.

The line ran a few feet, and he slowed it with the edge of his left hand, not grasping it, only letting the weight of his hand serve as a drag, keeping the fish from going out as rapidly as he might, holding against its downward rush, tiring it, making it spend itself to reach the deep of the river. He watched the line slash the water, away from a patch of hyacinths, then back toward it again. He wants to go for the roots, but he can't find the right place. They're too thick for him. He needs a passage. The fish darted downward, and he towed back on the line, easing it as he felt the pressure slide off to one side and the line move in a broad circle toward the open water.

Once there, it was easy. No gift greater than patience was required. The fish must be a young one. It had gone out into the open water halfway across the river where no maneuvering was possible. It had not headed directly toward the boat in order to slacken the line. Now he could feel the time between surges like the space that measures labor pains. Her first had been her last. Down there, with a small fire in its mouth, the fish was tiring. She had tired. Then, almost as suddenly as the bait has disappeared, the pull on the line fell off and he drew the slack in as quickly as he could, touching the automatic reel so that line would not pile up on the gunwale or in the bottom of the bateau. Maybe he's older than I thought. Or a fast learner. Here he comes.

The boat still lay in shadow a dozen yards from the shore. But the first rays of sunlight had begun to cut through the thin cover of trees to the east, to play on the thread of the river. So that when the bass broke water twenty yards from the boat, it leapt into a glory of first light. It twisted and shook its large head, the sun glinting and shimmering on the green-gold scales of its back and sides. As it fell back, he heard that sound as of a distant pistol shot, invisible concomitant of a bass leaping, whether at the end of a line or at an insect or small bird almost escaped. He could not remember when he had first heard it. He did not remember the sound of her sobbing, unable to speak. He did not remember that.

As the bass vanished again, he drew the line in quickly, feeling only last tentative darts this way and that, without plan or direction. He saw the long leader break the water then and pulled the line up beside the boat and reached into the water. He caught the bass by the lower part of its large mouth and lifted it carefully into the air. Once he had hold of the lower jaw and bent it down with the fish's weight, it was paralyzed temporarily. Water drained off it, and its dark, beautiful eyes glinted in the sun. He remembered like a gnomic prayer his father's admonition never to touch a bass with dry hands. It would cause a fungus that would kill the fish if you released it afterward. He did not remember the carmine moisture on her lips, dry final coughing. He lay the fly rod down lengthwise in the boat, and began to work the fly loose. It was caught in the muscle and bone in the upper part of the mouth, and the barb had to be backed out the tear through which it had entered. The muscle had been torn by the fight, and it was easy to inch the hook out. When it was clear, he held the bass up against the distant pattern of sun on the river, its life full and rich in his hands. Then, slowly, as if regretting, he lowered it back into the water and released it.

For a moment, the bass lay still, as if it had no memory of the water. Then, almost as quickly as it had taken the fly, it vanished back down there.

He paused and shook a cigarette out of the crumpled *Picayune* pack. He had been smoking for fifty years now.

They had become hard to find, even in Louisiana, by the 1960s. He had ordered them since then from a shop on the corner of Royal and Canal in New Orleans. Crashaw swore the Thing had arisen as a result of them. He had paid him no mind. There was another source for that. He had considered time itself, the anguish of watching the world sloughed away around him. Friends, customs, buildings, institutions lost. Other things. He did not remember the first time he had seen her. The wonder of. The cigarette smoke was burning his eyes, and he stroked the wine-colored water with his paddle, the slight motion carrying smoke away to dissolve in the shadows.

It was almost full light by then, and far down the river, around the bend toward Madisonville, he could hear a motor. At first it stuttered and choked off. Then it caught on, its pitch changing as it did so, and he shifted into gear. He pushed the bateau a few yards on, skirting a fallen log which had been sinking slowly into the river for years. For some reason, he had always associated the fallen tree with Laocoon, caught in the toils and folds of a serpent, perhaps named time. And, in recent years, with himself as well. He could remember when the tree had fallen, when he had had to draw in his line and set the rod aside in order to paddle around it. No, he thought. I go back before that. I remember before it fell. I can remember when it stood on the bank. It was before the war. Lightning. One night, and then it was dead, and it stayed that way for years. He did not remember telling her they called such a tree a widow-maker, her frown and sharply inhaled breath. When I came back from France, it was down. I asked Dexter. He said it was the late summer of 1943 while I was drinking Watneys bitter and waiting for what was coming.

As the log fell away behind, he thought of Judge Robert Edward L. Blakely, and his last trial. — Fish or cut bait, boys, the old man told them when they paused too long between questions. — You know what I got in here isn't going to wait on you. Anyhow, it's getting on to fishing time, and I be damned if I'm going to be here when the heat breaks. Call your next witness, counselor.

He blew smoke up into the cool air as the bateau drifted into shadow again. So many courtrooms, so many trials. So many compromises. He checked the long plastic leader of his line. It was still clear of nicks and solidly embedded in the main line. There was a good stretch of water ahead. He had caught many fish there over the years. The river did not curve, but it had cut deeply into the bank, stranding cypresses, which stood alone in the shallow water, providing places for the fish to nest or feed. But the wide lagoonlike place had to be fished carefully. He had to cast long, staying well away from the bank because the water was no more than two or three feet deep across the whole area, and he had learned as a youngster that a boat moving closer than the drop into deep water would clear the place of bass in a moment. It was a challenge to fish it well.

He remembered that they would gather in the judge's office at noon, the lawyers who had practiced with him and before him over half a century. They would bring their lunches and eat with him, some who had not carried a brown paper bag since they were children with a sack or a round tobacco can full of cold fried chicken and stale biscuits. They had simply begun to drop in one day, unplanned, undiscussed among one another. To pass the time.

Because the word had gotten out from Dr. Ishmael at the parish hospital. Terminal. Inoperable. Painful. Weeks. At the most, a few months. And their coming to lunch was more than tribute. It was that they wanted to be with him for as long as they could, and being lawyers, doubting all, out of an abundance of caution, they reckoned on no more time than each day provided. They would eat and laugh and drink illegal whiskey, sometimes the very evidence of a moonshiner's recent trial. It would be poured ceremoniously out of mason jars into water tumblers, while someone noted the incredible rate at which cases for the making of illegal whiskey tended to be dismissed in Judge Blakely's court. For lack of evidence.

— Well, Ed, the judge would say, — we got to enforce the law. But sometimes we need to retard it a little. If anybody on this sorry wheezing globe should know you can have too much damned law, we should . . .

They would laugh and tell stories on one another, implying every sin, recalling feverishly the old times, times the young lawyers would never see the like of: when the Old Regulars ran New Orleans as if it were a great lottery set up for their benefit, when Huey was governor, when he threatened to expropriate Standard Oil—which they knew and he knew he could not do, and yet . . . And when the courthouse clock struck one, they would rise without being bidden. The old man would rise last among them, and lift his tumbler filled to the brim for the third time in an hour. He would hold it aloft and say softly,

— Gentlemen, I give you Robert E. Lee.

— To Lee, the others would respond, and then, downing the balance of their drinks, file out into the cool, dark halls of the courthouse.

He could see them all now, the old and the young, standing in the musty chambers against the backdrop of buckram-bound lawbooks: *St. Martins Reports*, the *Louisiana Annual*, the *Southern Reporter*, *Orleans Appeals*, the *Annotated Civil Code*, copies of Planiol and the *Code Napoléon*, of Pothier and Laurent, and all the other written instruments by which they lived together. He could see them in his mind's eye, thirty-eight years gone now, the old long dead, the young old, standing as if in one of the engravings of the Mermaid Tavern, the *Signing of the Declaration*, or the *Solvay Conference of 1913*. His friends and brothers, the root and branch of his life. Yet not the flower because he would not see her, head thrown back, laughing, rain falling through sun, scintillating against the windowpane in that shotgun cottage where.

He had heaved up the motor and was paddling with his left hand, sometimes cross-paddling to hold the bateau close enough but not too close. Now he was casting the line in long graceful whorls that arched across the sky from the thread of the river behind into the lagoon ahead, barely missing the outstretched branches of the cypresses, falling soundlessly in the water, placing the yellow bug with its white rubber legs little more than six or eight inches from his target fifty or sixty feet away.

The sun was high now, almost midway above the river. The windless surface of the river was scattered with darts of light. Even so, there were shadowed places, bunched groves of cypress, oak, and gum growing in the water or thickly clustered along the bank, where the water ran dark even at noon. By now, the big fish had gone down, but there was always that odd one who swam his own way, kept his own hours. Ordinarily, fishermen went in about now, ate and lounged and waited for the heat to break, for the fish to rise and feed again.

I don't have that kind of time, he thought. What with the Thing working around the clock. Anyhow, I never *did* go in. I never did want that statistical fish. I wanted my own fish, and that crazy bastard just might sleep all night, get up at noon, work till three, and go down again. That's the one I wanted to see.

He smiled, thinking that he had probably put almost as many fish back into this river as he had taken from it. He took only what he could eat. He never gave fish away, and he never stored them in a freezer. When he ate them, they were caught to order. He did not remember her, arms wet with cooking oil, yellow with cornmeal, saying.

The end of the lagoon lay ahead, where the bank came back out, and the shallows measured no more than three or four yards. He had really not expected anything of it today. The sun was too high, and the water was too shallow. But sometimes, the younger bass, less affected by the heat, would move in there to feed, safe from jackfish and gar. They would hit the bait like giants. He loved to see them shake and twist, dancing on the sunny water. It occurred to him that these green-golden fishes had meant as much to his life as the course of the law. But even as he thought it, he laughed aloud. Because bass were as much a part of the law as he was, as were the courts in which he had passed his life, the attorneys with whom he had lived it out. The law is *lex*. The bass is *logos*. She was. He remembered a passage from one of the old Greeks, something about how deep lies the logos, so deep that no dive could reach it. You could not, deep-diving, find the depth of the soul, though you traveled the whole way down, so profound is its logos. That was it. And I'll know soon enough about that. There's so little way left to go now.

The insects were mostly in now. Mosquito hawks, june-bugs—all the mites that drew the fishes upward toward the light. They vanished under leaves, even into cracks in the bark of trees as the sun reached its height. They waited for that strong light to break and then, at dusk, they would begin to sound and feed and flit across the water once more in that cycle that bracketed late March to November.

At the end of the lagoon there was a space where raw soil had broken into the water, rootless, without grass or weeds. When there was a heavy rain, the wash-off flowed there. Then the bass would stand off a little to strike at the food carried to them by the flood. At any other time, there were no fish there, and so he drew in his line in order to move past, back into a clump of trees and marsh grass where frogs bred and the bass stalked like tigers. But the pain hit him then. As if someone had opened a door or raised a window shade, and agony looked in. It was not such a pain as to make a man moan. Rather to make him scream. Except that it had come so often lately that he only bent double in the boat, making it slosh from side to side in the water.

— Ahhh, he sobbed, holding to the gunwales. It was a sob because he knew always that the door, the shade was there, knew what lay behind it. He was accustomed to it. He was not used to it. You do not get used to pain that drives directly to what you had once taken for the center of your being and resonates there, thick with death, bright, awful chord steeped in the timbre of ageless loss. Each time it comes, it must unman you. Or take you away. As she lay dying, he had held.

He came to himself and raised up from the bottom of the boat. He took a bottle from his worn denim jacket. He threw down three of the small yellow tablets inside, washing them down with a handful of river water. The plastic bottle had a paper label curled up inside. It said, "For Pain. One Tablet Every Four Hours." But even Howard had admitted the absurdity of that. They had sat one evening in his office.

— Nothing, Dr. Howard Crashaw had told him. — Not a goddamned thing to be done. Oat-cell carcinoma. God couldn't cure it . . . No, that's wrong. That's a stupid medical technician's claim. *We* can't do anything. It's too fast. By the time there's enough to biopsy, it's off and running. Maybe it's the cost of what we do, what we are . . .

— All right, he remembered saying. — How do we handle it? This is the age of dope, isn't it? Should I just take some kind of consciousness-expanding thing and go out till it happens . . . ?

Howard had been astonished by the question. As if he had not been supposed to know about such things. Howard was a good doctor, and he shrank from what he did not know. He understood Howard's feelings. He was going to die, and soon. But Howard would live after. And what was now a mystery would, one day before long, become elementary. And Howard would think of him, and the vast parade of others who had gone before because he, Howard, could not then grasp what any intern could explain now.

He sat back in the boat smiling. The drug took effect almost at once. When he took three of them together, they did very well. You tended to wonder what trivial pain might be dealt with by one of them. There was a peculiar side effect he had hated at first that was still the prime reason he did not simply keep enough of the stuff in his system to stave off the pain altogether. It seemed to him that when he had taken enough of the pills, he could feel the Thing in him, working, moving from cell to cell, breaking loose in bits and flowing in the pressured stream of his blood to some new location to commence working again. Under the spell of the narcotic, it seemed he had an occupant rather than a disease, something dredging, probing inside him, seeking some sort of truth, which it could not find because he would not remember, destroying, rejecting the rest.

It was absurd, and he had come to look at the whole thing as a metaphysical conceit fostered by the drug. Still, to sense the Thing working eased nothing. He closed his eyes and breathed deeply then. He smelled the rich deepness of the water, amalgam of decay and generation, death and birth, fallen leaves and rotten logs. He picked up his rod and pulled in the rest of his line and paddled a little further, past the bald place on the bank.

As he did so, he touched the monofilament leader again, running his finger along it. If there were as much as a tiny nick in the line, it would part under pressure at far less than its test weight. You could not see the nicks the line

picked up from rubbing over a sunken log or a slight pro-
jection of rock or riprap. Sight was useless. You had to
touch, to test with your hands. As they had touched. The
line was sound, and he let it trail over the side as he
stroked farther on.

Past the wash-off, the bank hooked in again. Only here
the water was deep because this place was at the bottom of
a long slow curve in the river, and took the force of the
current when the water was high. The current would try
to flow straight, would burrow into this cul-de-sac, and
then straighten out and move on down toward the town,
farther on toward Pontchartrain. The place was a grove of
tall trees that had once been on the bank before the erosion
had taken it away and pushed it back. Most of the oaks
and gums had died. The willows had retreated to the bank
to wave softly above palmettos and scrub. But the cypresses
still stood, closed in together, their branches forming a
canopy over the whole area. There were even a few quak-
ing, oozy little islands supported by intricate tangles of
roots, composed of a little earth, decades' deposits of rotten
leaves and water plants. But, except for shafts of sunlight,
which pierced through where the trees were more widely
spaced, the whole grove lay in perpetual shadow. Even at
high noon, the fish could be seen swirling, striking toward
the back where the darkness faded into the bank itself.

He called this place Venus' arbor. He could not. Did not
remember. Why? Because this was the hardest place to
work on the river. It required great patience. It required
knowledge of the water. Because if you moved too quickly,
or without knowledge, you might go aground. To get off
again, you would have to make noise, and the sound would
carry all through the grove. The swirls and strikes would
vanish at once, as if nothing had ever been there. She had.
With. Him. He had to stifle a laugh of exultation. He did
not remember why. The pain was down for a little while,

and this was the good place. Where they had come. Away
from. Down in the bottom of the boat was a bottle. He
picked it up. It was wet from the tiny leakage that covered
the bottom of the bateau with perhaps a half-inch of water.
A famous first, he thought, studying the dripping label.
Old Overholt. Good solid rye whiskey. The best. Never
mind the young lawyers with their light scotch, their Black
Jack and Wild Turkey. No, this was of old. He remembered how they had customarily gone over to the little
restaurant across from the Gretna Courthouse after a trial,
the winner buying the loser as much whiskey as he could
drink, then paying for the cab home, or taking him there
yourself. Takes nothing from winning, Judge Blakely had
used to say, and makes a man consider losing as no worse
than second place. They always drank rye, chasing it
with Jax beer. During one bone-wracking murder trial, a
terrible case that stretched out over the better part of a
month, he and an assistant district attorney, despising the
trial and everything related to it, preempted the usual
custom and spent one long afternoon recess drinking together, handicapping the jury, betting on who would be
foreman. Afterward, they had gone back to court plain
drunk, spared lasting ignominy only by the fact that Judge
Blakely had come looking for them to discuss a motion,
and had stayed to have a few himself.

— Counsel will approach the bench, Judge Blakely had
directed when they had gotten back into court, weaving,
hardly able to find counsel's table.

The judge had leaned forward, waving away the reporter. — Boys, I'd entertain a motion for recess until
tomorrow, he said without a trace of expression. — I don't
know about you, but I can't count the damned jury.

— What jury? the assistant district attorney asked,
squinting.

Then the three of them—bone tired, sick of the trial, seeing no possibility of justice in it where killer and victim had together, over the years, constructed the bloody denouement—had gone back and drunk some more. And she had. Waiting afterward. So tired, but.

Now he was looking at the bottle again, paused beside a huge cypress. He had never taken a drink of hard liquor before when he was fishing. A little beer, perhaps. But not whiskey. No one who knew what he was about drank out on the water. The river was as beautiful as anything God had placed on the earth. But its logos was hard. It allowed no errors. A hand in the wrong place meant a cottonmouth bite. To reach up into a tree for a snagged bait without parting the branches first meant a hornet's nest would empty itself on you. Men died on the river every season because they were foolish or headstrong. Or because they drank. Drinking cost you the edge, and nobody could afford to lose the edge. Because no one knew the river. They only guessed. They surmised. Once he had run full tilt into a massive floating log and ripped out the bottom of his boat where no log had been ten minutes before. They knew this much: a barometer below thirty, an east wind, a recent bad rain, and there would be no luck. Most especially the east wind. God knew why. But why the Thing? God knows.

He opened the quart of whiskey, thinking: the first time in fifty years that he had ever so much as carried a bottle in his boat. His father had been death on it. He himself had lost an uncle to it. The river has rules, like the rules of court. Only more rigorous. And the people who live in such a water-riven state all know the rules. His housekeeper had looked at him strangely this morning when he put the bottle into the tackle box. Well, what about that, Mr. Sentell? I never seen you. If she was here.

He could not remember the rest of that sentence, and he opened the bottle quickly and drank deep. At this age it was good to break the rules. Because the rules were for the young. To preserve them for something else. He was beyond that. Time makes poets of us all. He grinned broadly. Now he could write his name in water. Or good rye whiskey. Deep-diving into time itself. Half a century is enough to hold to the rules. Most of his friends who had held to the rules till the last day were nonetheless dead. He thought, if I had a billion dollars, I couldn't reconstruct that scene, that picture with us all drinking in Judge Blakely's chambers. Lord, he thought, we're all commorientes. Every dying is contemporaneous with every other. Tulane law. Class of 1929. How many were left? He could see them all, strong, arrogant, assured, with an old city, a state awaiting their coming to the bar. But wait, he remembered thinking even then, his father and mother smiling, proud, blessing him for realizing in his own success the continuation of their hopes.

But wait. What about twenty, thirty, fifty years on? Her eyes sparkling, her kiss. Which he did not. Remember?

He took another drink and turned the boat ever so slightly so that it would point into the grove. Then he quickly back-paddled. No, he thought. Not now. I don't feel like it. There was a dry place, a place raised at the back of the grove, and there they had promised. No, I'll come back here later. When the sun is down. That's the best.

He moved on toward the mouth of a cut that led to the country club marina. It was wide and deep, cut back into the bank on a perpendicular. There was little growth down at the edge of the water, but there was a myriad of broken stumps and half-sunken logs. The fish there were mostly small, but the feed was good, and sometimes the large bass would move in there, eating small bream and goggle-eye. He knew of a corner where the white bass tended to swim

and feed. They were no good for a fight, but they made
better eating than anything beside the bream.

He felt the Thing rising again, that feeling of probing,
as if pain were a conscious entity looking for a place to
break through, to reduce him to a moaning cringing body
full of tubes on a hospital bed. Howard had said: When
it gets bad enough, you'll have to give in. Nobody can take
the last of it. We can make you comfortable. We can
goddamned sure do that . . .

Howard had turned away, and he had thought there were
tears in his eyes. He was touched. He had not thought that
the young doctor had liked him so much. Come on, Howard, you know better than that. I've been an uncomfortable
man all my life. I'll just keep coming back for more and
more dope, and you'll give it to me, pusher for super-
annuated lawyers . . .

They had laughed and had some drinks. And when they
had drunk enough, Howard told him he should find another
doctor, that he was no good. Howard said that he had tried,
but he was no damned good because he couldn't even master the very first thing about being a physician, which is
to see your patients as problems to be solved, equations to
be rebalanced. Howard had cried outright then, saying that
he had never lost a patient without losing some of himself,
that the worst was children, but that it was all terrible, and
that he was going to give it up and take what money he
had and buy a fishing camp somewhere or go back to divinity school and become an Episcopalian minister. Then,
drunk as a barroom cricket, Howard had mentioned another
patient. They both had known. He had spoken of her with
love, had said how. Her last.

He could not remember that. He took another pull on
the bottle and remembered his freshman year in law school.
He had done the Civil Law, but that year he had been
reading poetry. Oh my God, I haven't thought of poetry

in forty years. There had been a girl, he could not. Remember her name? He had written a poem for. Someone. The silliest possible thing. Writing. A poem. Suddenly he could even remember the name of one. He had written. Someone. Several poems. One had been *Viajera*. Voyager. That same time, he had worked on a law-review article. "The Civilian Law of Lease." Not poetry at all.

He found himself almost past the cut then and had to paddle backward to keep the current from driving him so far that he might have to lower the motor to get back. He could no longer paddle against the current in the river. That had bemused him. He could remember paddling six or seven miles against the current years ago. It had been easy. But not now.

With a few good strokes he left the river and entered the smooth water of the cut, past the roots and dead branches that lined the entrance. Perhaps twenty yards in, another cut went to the left. The cuts made a box, one branch, the one he was on, running back to the country-club docks, the other, the one to the left, turning back upon itself. In the middle was a raised section of land with a ten-foot levee around it. In there was a sludge pool which served as a giant septic tank for the tract of houses around the country club. Without plan, fish eggs had gotten into the ten- or twelve-acre pond, and the catfish especially had grown immense on the influx of human waste. None of the inhabitants, mostly yankees, would fish there. Local people, unconcerned about the fishes' diet, came frequently to catch enormous catfish, fat and tasty.

He leaned back against the canvas seat he had bought. It was the first support he had ever had. A compromise with the Thing. The boat rode now, tideless, almost unmoving, its only momentum that of his last thrust with the paddle. He sipped some rye and studied the place. The sun had just barely started down, and the air, warm before, had almost imperceptibly begun to cool. He had forgotten his watch, but it must be close to two. Things hurried in November. They had met. In November, the warmth faded, and twilight was brief. But it didn't matter. The whiskey provided all the warmth he could need. The pain was still seeking a way up, but it had not found it, not yet. In a little while, he would take some more pills.

— Now be careful. This is a morphine counterfeit, Howard had told him. Only it's at least a factor of five more potent. I mean, this stuff is terrific. No matter how bad . . . it gets, no more than two every two hours. Even that's dangerous. And nothing to drink. I mean, *nothing*. You could . . .

— Die? he had finished the sentence. — Hell, that would be a loss. Cut off in his prime . . . Shit, Howard . . .

Now he had to choose. Up ahead, along the way to the docks and slips, there was good fishing on both sides. Once, during a light spring shower, he had had seventeen strikes in twenty casts and had boated fifteen bass and bream just right for frying. It happened like that sometimes. But that was the straight way. It was where the smart fisherman went when things were right. To the left, the cut was narrower, closer, with willows and even a few cedars growing out over the water, and the better part of thirty years' rubble accumulated along the banks and in the water. It was very nearly impossible to use a fly rod in there because there was no back room, no space in which to let the line arch before you sent it forward toward its target. Almost no one fished that cut. It wasn't worth the trouble. The few who tried it always used a spinning rig. He let the bateau coast for an instant more. Then, with an almost demonic thrust, he dragged it into the left cut.

Things were even more quiet there. The slight wind that

had cooled him during high sun died, deflected by the shield of trees that rose suddenly and solidly along the bank there. And he remembered the poem.

> Voyager, we have caught a maze of
> dainty starlings spearing sun
> from out eyes' corners as we marched
> heads down and hearts askew.
>
> And voyager, we have marked each feathered
> renascence, bold matter skipping mad
> through quaint informal jays, secret
> journeys deadly swift performed by
> marble hawks.
>
> No wonder, earthbound, each of us must
> fret and string the long hot silent
> busy afternoon into fluttering dusk,
> a hope for music.
>
> > Our souls have made
> > poor matches; we are
> > darkling,
> > and the hollow of our
> > bones is filled with
> > dust.
>
> Shall the shape of morning, voyager, be
> that of delectable sparrows spangling
> your ears, dancing crystal figures
> in the shrill delightful air,
>
> or will you hasten with us into profitable
> day
>
> and limp by noon?

His eyes were closed as he remembered. Jesus Christ. Did I do that? Did I really? I guess I. Saw the love. When she had finished. Reading the shoreline, he began to reel out a short length of line. If you could handle a fly rod properly, you could do without the back space. All you needed was room enough to roll the line. You laid out a length, and kept your rod low, forcing the line into a circle, so that as it moved, the end would land almost as accurately as if you had cast in the ordinary manner.

Then he saw on the bank, among cypress, willow, and gum, a single camphor tree. He gave the bateau a single push and let it come into the bank. He reached up and drew down a handful of the leaves and pulled them off, crushing them in his hand as he did so. He closed his eyes and breathed deep, the pungent sharp odor of camphor filling his nostrils, almost a call back to the world. He felt tears spring up in his eyes. Nothing to do with anything. What? The hidden unconscious anguish of the body about to be parted from those things that moved it. Yes, only that. What he had wanted to say in the poem almost forty years ago. To Someone. That there was a part of him not bound to the law, or a child of rules and procedure. A part bound only by the bright sky and the deep water, the spring grass and the acrid odor of leaves burning in the fall. What she had found and loved as much as. He hated the inter-ruption, but the pain had found its way through, patiently, with a wealth of time in which to search. He shrugged, reached for the plastic bottle of pills, threw down another three—or was it four—and then washed them down with a shot of rye.

He held the bottle in his right hand and paddled with his left. He moved quickly into the overcast of the cut and began rolling his line. Almost immediately, he felt a touch on the yellow bait he could barely see in the shadows. He drew back and cast again. Nothing. And again. This time, the initial tug sustained itself, and he drew the rod upward, dodging the overhanging branches, pulling in line with his left, touching the automatic reel with the small finger of his right hand as he did so. The bottle was getting in his way. He was about to gather rod and line into his left hand in order to cap the bottle when the pressure on the line suddenly faded.

A goggle-eye, he thought. That's the way they always act. You get a solid hit, a short run. Then they fall off. They've got no fight in them. There was no reason to worry about the bottle. He could handle the goggle-eye still holding the bottle in his hand. You simply had to reel them in quickly, because if they managed to get some slack on the line, they might slip away. As he drew the line short, he saw the fish. Perhaps ten or twelve inches long, fat. A goggle-eye. He boated the fish which hardly struggled as he freed it from the hook. Then he pushed off with his paddle, and began to coast slowly down the slip again. He rolled the line up under the low-hanging branches. Suddenly, up ahead, in the thread of the stream, there was a roiling in the water. Perhaps fifty or sixty yards away. He smiled as he saw the shovel-head of an alligator moving toward the far bank. Even as his boat moved toward it, it paid him no mind. When it had reached the shore, it crawled from the water slowly, moving up the bank foot by foot. He watched it move. Water streamed down its sides. From where he sat, he could see the alligator's head in profile. The corner of its mouth seemed curled upward, as if it were grinning. As if to recall old mortality and the long dying fall of those who, long ago, had crawled up onto the shore never to return.

It was then that the pain surprised him, breaking through without the least warning. For the smallest portion of a second, he lost himself and thought. Of her. He concentrated on the pain, the richness, the texture of it as it moved across his chest, into his abdomen. Metastasis. Movement. The Thing was like a concerto within him, moving, surging, finding its own path from one place to another. He could not stand its rhythm, strumming across his wasted ribs, up into his throat. Almost remembering. Something more powerful, more awful than the pain threatened to break through. Dark hair, dark eyes. Dark water splashed as he shivered in the boat. He took two more pills, wondering if, on account of them, he might pass out. He had learned, to his surprise, that he had an incredible resistance to narcotics. Even Howard had admitted it one day when they had gone out for a few drinks. He had taken six pills in an hour. While he drank.

— An ordinary man would be . . . out. I mean, what the hell is with you, Bob?

He had smiled, leaned across the table, one eyebrow raised. — You are not dealing with an ordinary man, doctor. You are dealing with . . . Cancer Man . . .

The words had hardly been out before he realized that they were wrong. He did not need to see Howard's stricken face. He knew. There are things you cannot play with, even if they belong to you. He and Howard had never gone drinking again. It seemed ironic to discover when you are nearly seventy years old that you have not yet learned all the rules.

He cast again quickly, and another goggle-eye took the bait. He brought the fish in slowly, detached it from the hook, and stored it with the other in the bait well. He was casting rapidly now, hardly concerned where the bait might fall. That night. In Houston back from Austin, where they had spent their first night. Together with the descending sun, there was a rising breeze. Now he began to feel that it was deep autumn. The bug lighted beside a great sodden stump. He could not remember how long the stump had been there. He thought perhaps before his time. Because the broken tree that had once stood above it had surely vanished before he could remember. The memory of man runneth not to the contrary. Then, almost as quickly as the bug hit the water, it vanished. For a second, he wondered if possibly it had broken off the line. But then he felt a sudden and powerful downward tug and jerked back on the line quickly to set the hook. This could be the one. Every time he had walked into the court room and set down his briefcase he had thought, *this could be the one.* But none had been. That Great Case had never materialized. There had been many that brought him wealth. There had been some that had even become bench marks in jurisprudence. But not that one, the one that carried to the horizon, that changed what was to what would be. No, in his life, only she.

He frowned and held the line close. Not tight. Close. The distinction was elementary. It was the difference between a trust that something large and worthwhile was on the line, and the certainty that a small fish had hit that was worth no more time than might be required to draw him up and free him from the hook. Almost any fish might punch the line in that initial burst. Especially goggle-eye. They would hit hard and run well, and then suddenly collapse. But if the pressure of that first surge should continue, even grow stronger, what then? If you had not taken the first drive seriously, most often you lost the fish that pushed onward. Because the hook was not set. Because you had doubted, had assumed wrongly. But if you held closely at the first, you could manage things. To hold tightly was to lose the line to that fish that you had doubted.

The line cut sharply out from his left, from under the trees across the bow of the boat. He had to lean forward quickly with his body to make up for the slowness of his response with the line and the road, to keep the line from fouling under the boat. This isn't a goggle-eye. It isn't a small bass, he thought. This is something else like. Their first kiss. The Cotton Bowl. Oh dearest, I think I'm in love with. You come to sense the extraordinary when your hands and mind have spent enough time at a craft. He remembered that time. It boiled down to the final argument to the jury. His plaintiff crippled horribly. A cruel defense. The assumption of risk. Ladies and gentlemen. You are Art Clifford.

And this is what you did. Did you assume that risk? Given
that life, that experience, did you suppose things would go
that way? Because if Art assumed the risk, we all do.
Is this one of those risks we assume? It was dark and late.
He was utterly alone in his victory, opposing counsel youth-
ful, angry at his loss, refusing to go for drinks. He had had
a few by himself. She had come, her face expectant. Yes,
my love. One of the Great Days. Oh, sweetheart, let's go
and try. Try to think about this moment. This fish.
Love? You can't mean it.

He could not tell yet what he had on the line. Maybe
he had foul-hooked a good two-pound bass. A fish hooked
in the gills or along the back as it plunged at the bait seemed
much larger than one fair-hooked. He let the line run
through his fingers as slowly as he might. Every pound of
resistance tired the fish a little more. You resist as much as
you can. Once a federal judge had thrown a pencil at him
in anger. He had been very young, uncertain of what he
was about. O Lord, instruct thy servant. The line ran
through his fingers, and he began to feel the friction. Oh,
my dearest, it doesn't end. It is always there like an anthem.
Did Beethoven do a tenth symphony, Ode to Pain? The
weight on the line became greater and greater. It pulled on
his matchstick arms and began to pull the bow of the bateau
slowly back in the direction from which it had come. He
let line run, heard it stripping from the fly reel. The line
was twenty-pound test. It should hold.

The slow turning of the boat, the whiskey and the drugs
made him dizzy. He stroked the water with his sawed-off
paddle, holding for a moment rod and line in one hand.
It was a risky maneuver, but at the stern of the boat was a
nest of roots and broken branches. If the boat became
snagged there, the fish could use the weight of the boat to
break away. The boat broke clear, and he dropped the
paddle into the bottom of the boat, quickly reaching for the

loose line with his freed hand. Even as he did so, he could feel the strength of the fish down there. Then, in an instant, the line went dead. Not simply limp, loosing its tautness. Dead. He dragged it in with his left hand and the automatic reel pulled it in even more quickly than he could reel, but not matter how much line he could draw in, there was no feeling in it. Dead.

He leaned back in the boat, his back against the canvas seat. Gone. It had to be a good one. Gone. What the hell. That's what it means to come out here, he thought. Then, even as he relaxed, the line went taut again, and more than that, almost burned his hand as it ran out.

Christ, it's still on, he thought. It's fixing to come up now. It's a monster. It might even be a gar. Too much for a bass. It had never been his house, it was what she had wanted. Uptown. He had wanted a place on water. Where he could keep in mind the movements of the moon, the pulling of the tide. He had watched her instead.

Then almost fifty yards out, nearly on the other side of the cut, the fish broke water. It did not spring into the air like the two- and three-pounders. It was much too large. Rather it rolled, tossing its enormous head to rid itself of the tiny fly hook, which had become embedded in its jaw. It was dark green above, and as it rolled out beyond the shadowy trees, he could see the off-white glint of its belly. It had to weigh over fifteen pounds. He had seen ten- and twelve-pound bass over the years, though he had never caught one even that size. This one was bigger. It rushed at the shore like a torpedo. It actually leaves a wake, he thought. My God, what a fish.

It struck the bank blindly, twisted almost back upon itself, and went down again, headed this time up the cut toward the dogleg to the right, which led to a dead end clogged with brush, fallen logs, and dead branches. The fish couldn't know about that rubble. It was almost a quarter of a mile away, he thought. Then he thought again. Unless it lives in there, under the rubbish. They like that kind of cover. Especially the big ones, the old ones who have lived forever.

The boat moved slowly as the fish dragged against the line. I never knew a fish to fight like this. He's moving an eighty-pound boat with a two-hundred-pound—no, a hundred-and-thirty-pound—man in it. His eyes clouded, and the pain burned up and through like a tiny sun in nova. He almost dropped the rod, but habit made him grip it and the line in one hand. He reached once more for the pills and washed two down with whiskey. Then he sat waiting for the Thing to be pressed down again, the flame of pain quenched for a little while.

Now the bateau was at rest. He was tired. His head was swimming a little from the drugs and liquor. For the smallest fraction of a moment he wondered if he should try to horse the fish in. Or cut the line. He was very tired. But that was no way to leave things. Her lips had been. Rich and warm, the sun was settling toward the horizon. There would be no more than another hour of light. Probably a good deal less. He would catch the fish. There was no reason now to preserve his strength. He looked down at his wasted arms where the sleeves of the jacket had been pulled back as he worked the rod. He could see the outline of his thigh bones sharp against the cloth of his work pants.

Then the line rose and the boat began to move again, taking his mind off what was happening to him. The boat had almost reached the dogleg by now, and he tried to draw in a little line. A cloud passed across the sun, and he noticed for the first time that rain clouds were moving in from the north.

Now maybe I really should cut the line, he thought. As he pulled on the line, there was an answering opposite tug from below. War with a submarine. And maybe the fish was stronger now. He could feel the trembling in his arms and legs, in his hands. But the pain had subsided and he was all right now. There was plenty of whiskey left, and he possessed a wilderness of pills.

As the boat turned into the right angle at the dogleg, he heard the first drops of rain begin to fall on the water. It sounded as if someone were dropping kernels of rice onto paper. Rice in her hair, the veil. He raised the canvas seat a little and pulled out his poncho. He pulled it over his head before the rain reached his boat. Down the length of the cut, he could see the pile of broken timber, limbs, branches, and brush that marked the end of the water. If you left your boat and walked overland perhaps ten yards, you found yourself close to the boat docks and slips at the head of the main cut.

The fish did not relax its pressure, and he knew that if it was headed for the brush pile, and if it could reach it, there would be no chance of landing it. It was time to do some horsing. He shook a cigarette out of the crumpled pack, and struck a kitchen match against the side of the boat. He took a long pull on it and began putting more pressure on the line. He was surprised to feel the boat slow. Another pull, and some of the line came in. He touched the automatic retrieve and wound in the excess line before it could get tangled in the boat. The trembling in his arms had stopped, and he leaned forward. The rain was falling softly, regularly, and the clouds had all but effaced the sun. It was going to be dark soon now.

Old brother, he thought as he continued to draw in the line, you don't want to be drawn into the element above, no matter that you're heavy with years and feeling the change of water temperature more all the time. I'm hooked, too. They're fishing for me. I have to go. We all do. We can't stay in our element. We're not meant to stay here. They draw us up.

The line eased still more, and he found that he was pulling it in almost as fast as the retrieve could handle it. He felt a tentative probe from the pain, but it was only a distant landscape, uninteresting; present, but of no moment. Then he saw the fish.

At first he thought it was dead. For a bass it was immense. He had never seen one so large. As he drew it toward the bateau, loglike, twisting and twisting, he wondered if he could pull it aboard even if there was no fight left in it. When he got it alongside, he could tell that it was still alive. The eyes were dark, beautiful and dark as the water. The eyes of a dead bass turn quickly to a bright incongruous gold. It was at least six or eight inches across the back and as he peered down on it, he saw its gills moving slowly, fanlike, sweeping the dark water. It wasn't dead. It was simply tired. The bass was very old and had fought itself out. Against great odds. For a long time. In the room with her. Wasted and tired. An old woman now, and. He came to himself still staring at the fish. He could not get his net around it. It looked to weigh close to thirty pounds. But bass don't reach thirty pounds. He did not remember those last hours. She.

He reached down into the water with both hands and caught the big fish by the lower jaw. In a single motion, he lifted it into the air. He held it sparkling aloft, the dying light making of it a great shadow-fish against the darkening clouds. Then, of a sudden, its weight was oppressive and his arms too weak to support it longer.

He lowered the fish back into the water. Quickly, he leaned over the side of the boat and worked the bait loose. It was easy to do, and he enjoyed the quickness and clarity of his work. You can still do something right, you heap of old diseased rubble, he thought.

Now he fumbled for the rye whiskey without looking for it and took a long drink. Down in the water, the bass lay unmoving. Oh darling let me go. Let me. I only hate to leave. You. Could see the fish revive. Its tail moved suddenly, and it dived deep, its bulk vanishing from his sight in the broken surface of the water where the rain fell.

Then it was dark, and when he came out of the cut, he felt the full force of the wind that always blew along the river, whatever the season. He edged the bateau against the shore at the mouth of the cut, in the cover of a magnolia tree so tall and full that the rain did not penetrate it. Among the leaves at its base, he found some twigs and brush and branches still dry. He piled them up and made a fire. Then he cleaned the goggle-eyes and cooked them in a skillet with cornmeal and grease he had brought.

When he was done, the rain had stopped, the clouds broken, and the sky was clear. The moon was beginning to rise, and it had never looked so large and yellow. He had trouble balancing when he stood up. Hours in the boat makes you lose a sense of the land, he thought. For a little while its very solidity is alien, and the perpetual movement of the water is in your veins. He was very tired now, and the pain had begun to come back, waves against a collapsing shore. Still, when he had cleaned up, he stood awkwardly and pissed into the fire, watching with boyish pleasure as the flames died under his water.

He took up what was left of the fifth of rye and studied it against the rising moon. Then he took a few more of the pills and drank down the rest of the whiskey. The bottle of rye was empty. So was the bottle of pills. Things had come out even. He tossed the bottle toward the sky, watching childlike as it arched across the stars and fell with a soft sound into the river. For a moment, as he climbed back into the boat, he felt young and strong again. He left his rod and tackle and the rest of his equipment behind, taking only his paddle. The boat moved out onto the broad plane of the river.

Then he was looking for that certain place again, the grove where he had not fished this afternoon. Where he had not fished for almost nine years. He did not. Would not. Remember why? He saw the inlet canopied by tall cypresses out there ahead of him. Above, the Milky Way arched over him, a path of stars that seemed to plunge to earth within the grove ahead. It was a place where. He paddled slowly, paying no attention to the darkness, seeing Venus glowing in the sky, constant, asking him to remember.

Now the grove arose from the darkness, separated itself from the undifferentiated bulk of the shore's darkness, a configuration of trees and floating plants like no other. At the back, far back from the open water, there was a place. Where the land rose inexplicably and became solid, more than a mass of roots and rotting leaves. Where even on a dark night, the air crisp and chill, one could find. Her eyes had been closed. I know, she told him, setting sun touching her uncovered breast, why this is your favorite place.

He could feel the tears coursing down his cheeks. — The fishing is good, he said aloud, hearing his words flow in the darkness like the river.

— I know, he heard her laugh from beyond the shadows.

He remembered then, and the weight of loss was nothing compared to the memories.

Crushing out the anguish of losing her had distorted everything else. He felt tears on his cheeks, mourning not so much the losing as the time wasted not remembering.

In the chill night he stood up as the boat left the current and drifted into the utter darkness of the grove. Mist was rising there, whirling across the shattered stumps, skipping between the tranced and silent trees. He was amazed to find that the moon's light penetrated even there and made the still water glisten like a ballroom floor. He stretched out his arms and she was in them, his arms strong and full once more. Out there above the moon, he could see the plane of the galaxy itself, path of heaven, as the boat skewed and turned slowly to the music of nightbirds and crickets. The Pleiades, a starry court, snared his eyes, whirling, turning, and she, judges, advocates, all the suppliants found at last their logos and their meaning.

So that when the boat struck a cypress knee there in the quiet pool, he could not quite judge the motion of the distant stars or the touch of the autumn night from that of the dancing tree-crowns, that of the cool beloved water that sustained his fall, summation of yearning and pain. A court adjourned, another opening.

The Great Pumpkin

Mr. and Mrs. Twitty were retired. That is, Mr. Twitty was retired. Mrs. Twitty had nothing to retire from.

They had come to Belle Isle to enjoy life. They had that coming. So many years really *not* enjoying life, only looking forward to enjoying it. They had lived in Pittsburgh, Pennsylvania, and no one enjoyed living there.

Mr. Twitty had traveled in rainwear for forty years. He sold raincoats and galoshes in Ohio, New Jersey, Pennsylvania, Indiana, and a small piece of Illinois. Whenever anyone asked him what he did for a living, Mr. Twitty had a naughty thing he told them. Mrs. Twitty always blushed if she were there, no matter how many times he said it. People would always laugh and nudge each other, but Mr. Twitty would only smile.

They had a little cottage at the end of Humming Bird Lane in Paradise Villa. It was a nice little house with ivy and some honeysuckle growing around the door. It had belonged to an old maiden lady who had died of cancer without any relatives and it had sold cheap. Mr. and Mrs. Twitty had been lucky to get it, and they knew it.

During the day, Mr. Twitty would putter around the house or walk down to the artificial lake and go fishing. When he did, he always caught something because it was a well-stocked lake kept exclusively for Paradise Villa residents. But he never kept anything that he caught, because as a matter of fact he didn't like fish. They never had fish. He didn't know if Mrs. Twitty liked fish or not, but he supposed she didn't.

While he puttered or fished, Mrs. Twitty would spend her time in the kitchen or cleaning up. They had a very strict schedule of meals, with the same dishes at lunch and dinner each day of the week. The menu was made up of dishes Mr. Twitty liked, and every Monday's lunch and dinner was like every other Monday's. It was the same every other day, except that sometimes on Sunday, Mrs. Twitty would fix up a surprise. There was really nothing to clean up at all, but Mrs. Twitty tried anyhow, looking in the most remote and out-of-the-way places for dirt. When, as would occasionally happen, she came across a pocket of dust or grit, she would smile and attack it with Top Job or Mr. Clean and enjoy herself immensely.

They had never had any children, the Twittys. Not that they hadn't wanted them. They had. But one doctor spoke of a deformed uterus and another of low sperm-count, but all their expectations and talk didn't make babies and none had ever come. They were sorry, the Twittys. It was just too bad.

Because they loved children. One of the nicest things about Belle Isle was that there were lots of families with children. At Christmas, the smaller ones would go from house to house singing carols, carefully herded along the cold winding streets of Paradise Villa by a mother who had volunteered to do so the previous year in the glow of the children's sweet innocent chirping. They would ring the bell and warble "God Rest Ye Merry Gentlemen," in a loose, quavering, off-key way all their own. It was nice to see them, and it gave a special meaning to the Holy Season. Mr. Twitty would smile, almost embarrassed as the children sang. Mrs. Twitty would sigh. They did not talk about the children afterward. Mr. Twitty would turn on the television and they would watch a movie or a comedy show, sitting in their chairs close beside one another.

The older children were rougher, noisier, and not very polite. Some of them had motorbikes or cars and would roar up and down the streets in the evening, wrecking the silence and the peace of Paradise Villa. The local newspaper frequently editorialized about the lack of firm discipline and steady goals among American youth, but it never mentioned much by way of specifics, and the children of Belle Isle were never pointed out as examples.

Now it was October. There was a crisp pleasant chill in the air, and folks like the Twittys were looking forward to Thanksgiving and the holidays. But first there was that holiday especially for children—the spooky exciting time of Halloween. The Twittys especially liked Halloween because it gave them a chance to plan and prepare surprises for the kids. And they liked to watch the Charlie Brown television special about the Great Pumpkin.

The Great Pumpkin, Mr. Twitty said, was that wild exciting event that everybody aways looks forward to, waits for, hopes for in his life. Something different and wild and maybe even dangerous. But something special. Mrs. Twitty's eyes got large as she listened to him, because Mr. Twitty never talked that way. It put her in mind of a time, long ago, when Mr. Twitty was gone to Philadelphia and she had met a man at the May Company department store, and they had talked, and he bought her lunch and asked her to go with him to his hotel. He was a traveling salesman like Mr. Twitty and was only in town for a day or two. The strangest part was that she could not actually remember either what she had said or done. She was confused, because often, especially when lonely or blue, she would fantasize that she had smiled, touched his hand, said yes, and gone, and that they had sinned together, wildly, madly. But she suspected that this was not memory, really, but just fantasy. Anyhow, she smiled inwardly, *that* had been her Great Pumpkin.

So they waited till the 30th of October and then Mr. Twitty candied apples while Mrs. Twitty baked brownies and they cooked up some lovely chocolate candy together. It was a clear sunny day, and while the brownies baked, Mr. and Mrs. Twitty walked down to the store. Mr. Twitty was still talking about the Great Pumpkin. He said that, traveling on the road, he had often pretended that, at one stop or another, someone in authority would say, — Well, Twitty, you're a real goer. I like your style. Now we've got a little deal set up, and . . . But it had never happened. Only once, someone he could not even remember had sold him a $200 interest in an oil well they were drilling near Amarillo, Texas. He had never even heard what came of it. Maybe they never drilled it, or maybe they did and hit water. Or maybe they gushed all over west Texas, made 10 million dollars, and just never let him know. But the Great Pumpkin had never come along, and probably, Mr. Twitty smiled wisely, even if it had, it would have surely turned into a giant rutabaga.

Mrs. Twitty smiled and tried to remember the name and face of *her* Great Pumpkin, but she couldn't, and when Mr. Twitty made his joke about the rutabaga, she laughed right out loud right there in the supermarket. Not so much about the rutabaga, as for not being able to remember what her Great Pumpkin had been like.

When they got home from the store, it was evening. They took cellophane of various colors, ribbons, and a number of small toys made in Hong Kong and began to make up little parcels for the children. Mr. Twitty paused and tacked up skeletons and black cats and witches and bats made out of pasteboard in the foyer and on the front door. By bedtime, everything was ready, and Mr. and Mrs.

Twitty fell asleep talking softly of how much fun it would be next evening when the little ghosts and goblins came trick-or-treating.

The next day seemed very long. It was downright strange. Almost as if there were some indescribable tension between Mr. and Mrs. Twitty, although of course there wasn't. And they didn't talk all morning, and at lunch—it was Tuesday, and so Campbell's Golden Mushroom soup—they just ate quickly and nibbled their Dutch Rusk and then went off again: Mrs. Twitty to dust furniture she had dusted the day before; Mr. Twitty for a walk he really didn't feel like taking. The sun was already low and no one was on the streets. The trees were mottled gold and red, leaves beginning to fall like so many lovely coins scattered down the cold dismal streets. Once Mr. Twitty saw something dark flit through a stand of pine trees in a vacant lot he was passing. He laughed aloud at his instant's fright. Never too old, he thought, almost taking pleasure at the vestige of childishness still stored inside his aging body.

Mrs. Twitty was sitting alone in the parlor in front of the vacant television screen when he got home. The house was very warm, and Mr. Twitty almost felt faint. His nose itched. Somebody coming, he thought. Mrs. Twitty's whatnot, each shelf covered with tiny glass animals he had sent her over the years from so many dull towns, caught the last sunbeams, broke them into colors, and broadcast feeble tendrils against the mirror over the fireplace. Like a light show, Mr. Twitty thought. He was up on things, and had seen something on the television. Then the swirl of colors faded and vanished, and Mr. Twitty sighed as he took off his heavy sweater.

Mrs. Twitty's hands were folded in that certain way she had when she was nervous or tense. Sometimes she would begin talking when she felt that way, talking almost at random, saying nothing, really, just going on. But not this

time. She just sat while Mr. Twitty hung up his sweater
and turned on the evening news.

It was awful, of course. It always was. War and hunger,
pride and bigotry. Morals going, customs already gone.
Crime up, prices up. As if the end of the world Billy Gra-
ham preached was coming inevitably closer and closer
with nobody and nothing able or willing to hold it back.
Mr. Twitty wondered if maybe Jesus come again was going
to be everybody's Great Pumpkin, and then wondered
at his own crazy thought.

— Almost time for the Great Pumpkin, Mr. Twitty heard
himself say aloud.

Mrs. Twitty felt a chill travel up her spine as he said it,
and couldn't imagine why, thinking at the same time that
it was odd, what with all their talk, neither of them had
thought to buy a pumpkin and carve a jack-o'-lantern
out of it.

— Yes, Mrs. Twitty said after a while. — They'll be coming anytime now.

And they did. They came in threes and fours and half
dozens and once in a group of at least fifteen. They would
ring the doorbell and shriek in loud tiny piping voices,
— Trick-or-treat, trick-or-treat, whreee...!

Each time they did, Mr. and Mrs. Twitty would exchange a smile, get up from the television, turn down the
volume, and go to the door. Just inside, in the foyer, there
was a nice little table Mr. Twitty had bought at an exclu-
sive antique shop in Sandusky, Ohio, and had sent to Mrs.
Twitty after he had done something really awful at a
buyers' convention in Youngstown. On the table they had
placed the little parcels, and when Mrs. Twitty opened the
door, Mr. Twitty would quickly count the number of
youngsters and pick up enough parcels for them. He would
hold them while Mrs. Twitty took one at a time and handed
them to each costumed child with a smile and a kind word.

All kinds of twilight and midnight folks turned up in miniature form: devils and caterpillars, spidermen and cat-women, tiny pigs and lank clowns, outlaws and ruffians, galley slaves and hottentots, mad scientists and magicians. There was an anthology from zoos, graveyards, alchemist's garrets, abandoned castles, sewers and bell towers, opium dens and witches' hovels. It was as if all the forgotten and ignored of the earth, from the past, the present, the future, beasts, men, myths and nightmares, all had risen to go abroad on this one night to remind the ordinary world and the sleepwalkers in their homes of what they would most like to forget.

It went on for three or four hours, and then only a few came, and finally there was a long lull. The late news came on, repeating the stories told earlier, or at least telling stories just like them. Then it was bedtime. Mr. Twitty rose, stretched, turned off the television and the floor lamp and started toward the foyer. The table was almost empty. Only five or six of the little parcels were left. Just as he touched the light switch, there was a roar outside, as if all the motor-bikes in Belle Isle had come blasting to a stop right in front of Mr. and Mrs. Twitty's house. Almost at once, there was a hammering on the door, and as Mrs. Twitty came into the foyer, both of them heard a flurry of voices outside howling, — Trick-or-treat, trick-or-treat.

Mrs. Twitty was tired, but she put her smile in place, and Mr. Twitty picked up the remaining parcels, and Mrs. Twitty opened the door.

Out there they saw a gorilla, a skeleton, a cowboy, and a spaceman.

The Gorilla was large and hulking and threatening. Mrs. Twitty drew her breath in sharply when she saw him. He was covered with dark, moth-eaten fur, and his face was frozen in an expression of insane and insensate fury or lust or hatred or anguish, or a mixture of them all. His eyes were so deep-set that they were almost invisible, simple pits in which something like madness burned.

The Skeleton was very convincing. It looked like the very spirit of death itself, each bone articulated against the blackness of some fabric behind, and shimmering with what appeared to be some kind of phosphorescent paint. The Gorilla grunted and chuffed evilly; the Skeleton made no sound at all.

The Cowboy wore purple jeans, a shirt covered with fancy silver scrollwork, a bandana around his neck, a Stetson, and a mask. All but the jeans and the scrollwork were black, and Mr. Twitty wondered if western outlaws had looked like that when they went out to work. You could see only a little of his face beneath the mask, but what you *could* see looked rough and mean, and gave the Twittys no reason to want to see the rest.

Behind the others, the Spaceman wore a white uniform-like coveralls, only they were very tight and molded to his body. Around his head was a plastic helmet that looked for all the world like a fishbowl. The face inside was unmemorable, even-featured, characterless, the face of no man and every man—as if it had been issued by some government agency that would hold him responsible for its condition when it was returned. On his right shoulder, the Spaceman wore an emblem, and it confused Mr. Twitty, because right where Neil Armstrong had worn the American flag, this Spaceman wore an iron cross.

As the Twittys watched them, they all watched the Twittys.

— Took you long enough to answer, the Cowboy drawled. — You hard of hearing, pops?

Mr. Twitty didn't know what to say. He half-offered one of the parcels to the Cowboy, realizing even as he did how absurd the gesture was. The Spaceman saw this motion and his discomfiture, and laughed. It was a strange distant sound,

hollowed and muffled by the plastic helmet. As the Spaceman laughed, the Gorilla pushed forward, past Mrs. Twitty,
and into the foyer. The others followed behind him.

— Listen, Mr. Twitty was saying, still off-balance, uncertain of what to say or do.

— We're listening, we're listening, the Spaceman assured
Mr. Twitty from a long way off as the Gorilla eyed Mrs.
Twitty closely and then moved on into the parlor. — We
just got to use your phone, he said.

The Skeleton closed the door and put its blank white skull
close to Mr. Twitty's face. It tried to grin; the supple
mask warped into a terrible leer.

By the time Mr. Twitty had gotten himself together and
realized how outrageous all this was, the Cowboy was on
the phone dialing. As he waited for an answer, he took out
a cigarette and lit it. It was thin and brown and fat in the
middle, and looked a good bit like the roll-your-owns Mr.
Twitty had smoked as a young man. After a long drag, the
Cowboy passed the cigarette to the Gorilla who did the
same and held the smoke in his terrific lungs and rolled his
eyes and he handed the cigarette on to the Skeleton.

— Whew, the Skeleton coughed.

— Hello, Annie, the Cowboy barked, exhaling the smoke
at last. — It's The Kid. What you got on? I got three studs
over here, and we're all so horny we honk. Can you all
handle us? Huh? Lord yes we got dope. We got stuff you
can smoke, drop, shoot, sniff, line. Hell, honey, I got some
new stuff you can just look at and go . . .

Mrs. Twitty's smile wasn't gone yet—only fading, but
it was in poor repair. She wasn't sure what the Cowboy was
talking about, but somehow she felt it had to do with the
world that kept coming toward hers in the evening news.

— All right, Annie. Sure. Okay.

The Cowboy read off the Twittys' phone number, and
said he would wait for her call. He told Annie it was a mat-

ter of life and death that she clear out a little space, because it was gash or go down tonight.

The Gorilla and the Skeleton had seated themselves in Mr. and Mrs. Twitty's chairs and turned on the television. The Spaceman stood near the sofa with an odd sneer on his face. He had had his turn with the cigarette and now you could hardly see his unexceptional face for the mist of smoke swirling in his helmet.

— You boys have got to . . . Mr. Twitty began, but the Gorilla roared at him, waving its hairy arms and looking horrid. Mr. Twitty held his chin firm, but didn't finish what he wanted to say. It was the first time he had really felt old, too old to face things like this blasted gorilla—although, in fact, he had never faced much of anything even in the army, where he had worked in supply. The Cowboy sucked on his smoke again and sauntered over to Mr. Twitty, walking as if they were both in an old western bar.

— Pops, the Cowboy said, his mouth almost unmoving below the mask. — Whyn't you all just sit down and do your evening Bible-reading or whatever you do to pretend you're still groovin'? We got to wait for this call, okay?

Mr. Twitty was about to say, no, it wasn't okay at all, but he felt the pressure of Mrs. Twitty's hand on his arm, and he said nothing. He felt a sudden surge of love for his wife course through him, something positive and real, more than habit, that he had not felt for years. She was concerned about him, and somehow knowing that made the nasty deep taste of fear in his throat much easier to bear. He could stand on his dignity now; she had released him from the necessity of acting.

— All right, Mr. Twitty said, almost easily. — Just for the call.

The Spaceman laughed distantly, a nasty laugh. — Thanks, he said from a long way off: — Thanks a lot.

The Gorilla was laughing at one of Johnny Carson's more inane double entendres. Maybe the Skeleton was, too. How could you tell?

— Hey, mumsy, the Cowboy suddenly asked Mrs. Twitty. — You got any Southern Comfort?

Mrs. Twitty didn't know what to say. But her ravaged smile brightened ever so slightly.

— We've always loved the South, she began hesitantly. — That's why we moved here from Pittsburgh, Pennsylvania, and we never . . .

— Aw, you stupid cunt, I mean whiskey, the Cowboy cut her off. — Where the fuck are you people at?

Mrs. Twitty's lower lip trembled. — We . . . don't have any whiskey, she began again. But they were ignoring her now.

Mr. Twitty felt his ears and scalp growing hot. He had never heard that kind of talk before a lady, least of all Verna, Mrs. Twitty.

— Now listen, I want you to watch yourselves, he began, but before he could say anything else, the Gorilla had swung around in his chair and hit him with something large and heavy. The blow sent Mr. Twitty sprawling across the room, and when he managed to clear his head of what at first he thought was a ringing in his ears, but which was actually Mrs. Twitty screaming and screaming, he saw that the Gorilla had some kind of gun and that the Skeleton was hitting Mrs. Twitty with his fists over and over again, that her face was cut, and that the Skeleton was making some kind of strange high sound in its throat.

Mr. Twitty tried to climb to his feet to help Mrs. Twitty, but as he did, the Cowboy kicked him right in his privates, and Mr. Twitty went down again with a blinding, gut-ripping pain he had not felt in forty years. He must have passed out, because when he came to himself again, everything had changed. The Gorilla was still watching television all right, but the Cowboy was handing him another cigarette and was sitting in Mr. Twitty's chair. The Spaceman was just resettling his helmet and passing a bottle of Jack Daniels to the Skeleton, who now sat on the sofa next to Mrs. Twitty and had stopped beating her. When the Skeleton had slugged down a half-pint or so, it handed the bottle to Mrs. Twitty, who took a long pull on it almost matter-of-factly, as if she had been doing it for a long time.

Mr. Twitty wondered how long he had been unconscious, but as he tried to move, another blitz of pain shot through him and he moaned out loud for a pain that no man his age should have to suffer. When he looked again out of the mirage of his pain, the Cowboy was handing Mrs. Twitty one of those cigarettes. And she was taking it.

— Goddamn, Mr. Twitty heard himself say, but nobody paid any attention. The Skeleton was smoking and the Cowboy was with the Gorilla again, and they were watching the late movie, something about things from another planet. The Spaceman was out there laughing.

— Hey, old honey, the Cowboy called over his shoulder, — That old goof ever ball you any more?

Mr. Twitty tried to turn back to see Mrs. Twitty's face again, but even turning his head was pure agony.

— Ball . . . ? Mrs. Twitty said in a voice soft and filmy as if she were wearing a space-helmet, too.

— Screw, honey. You know. Intercourse?

— Oh, Intercourse.

The Gorilla threw up his paws and coughed and roared. As he did so, Mr. Twitty could see the gun in his lap. It was a sawed-off automatic shotgun. Mr. Twitty could tell, because it was just like an old Remington he had had when he was younger, except without much barrel, and hardly any stock at all.

It went on like that, the smoking and drinking for what seemed a long time from where Mr. Twitty was lying. Once he wondered where they had gotten the whiskey, and what the cigarette made them do, but this drifted out of his mind again as did the picture of Mrs. Twitty drinking and smoking with them. What would they do if she refused? The Cowboy was talking about the James Gang, and the Spaceman said something about Moondog. The Gorilla growled about the Animals, and even the Skeleton whispered a name that sounded like the Grateful Dead. Mr. Twitty heard all this pass in and out of his mind, and he thought he must be going crazy, but he was beginning to come out of it a little, and found that he could, if he was careful, move again. Then the Cowboy was smoking and saying things about sex and none of it made any sense at all.

The telephone rang. The Spaceman caught it, listening for a moment with the receiver up against his helmet. Then he hung up.

— No dice, the Spaceman said hollowly.

— Shit, the Skeleton croaked, almost aloud.

— Ain't that just too goddamned bad, the Cowboy muttered. — No way?

— What she said, the Spaceman answered.

The Gorilla kicked in the television screen, and the room went dark, sparks flying everywhere. The Skeleton threw the almost-empty bottle of Jack Daniels at the mirror over the fireplace. The Spaceman turned over the whatnot, and all of Mrs. Twitty's little glass animals crashed and tinkled to the floor. The Cowboy unzipped his jeans, went over to the sofa, ripped off Mrs. Twitty's skirt and underthings and began raping her. She squealed, but it was a funny sound, and the horror that flooded Mr. Twitty wasn't just the kind of horror he might have expected only a few hours ago.

And he could hear the Cowboy:
— Yipee, the Cowboy was yelling. — Aw-haw. Round 'em up, head 'em out . . .
And he could hear when the Cowboy was finished, and then the Skeleton. And the Spaceman.
The Gorilla got up from Mrs. Twitty's chair where he had been sitting staring at the shattered television screen. The gun in his lap slid down his furry thighs and landed on the floor as his huge paws fumbled with his hairy crotch, revealing parts just like those of a human being.
Mr. Twitty turned his head. He couldn't help it. There was no more deadly pain to use as an excuse for not seeing. He had to. He heard the Skeleton whispering how great it was to be dead, and the Spaceman said he was spaced out. The Cowboy told them it was all Dodge City, and no shit. The Gorilla was mounting Mrs. Twitty, pawing her, burying his huge head in her naked breasts and grunting and growling. Mr. Twitty saw this, and saw Mrs. Twitty's small pale hands caught in the Gorilla's thick roan fur.
He turned away. His eyes moved over the shadowy alien landscape of the parlor lighted only by the distant light in the foyer. He saw the blasted television screen, Mrs. Twitty's chair turned over, the parcels of candy and brownies and toys lying where he had dropped them.
And he saw the shotgun where it had fallen from the Gorilla's lap as he got up to go to Mrs. Twitty.
It took a long time to crawl that far. More than all his sixty years and more still. It was as if he had been crawling all his life, trying to cross that cold parlor floor, trying to reach that sawed-off shotgun. Could it be that those thousands upon thousands of miles he had driven in sun and rain, twilight and dawn, determined to get the job done, the sales quota filled and then some, had all been some kind of silly rehearsals for this? Well, why not? What else had those miles meant? Because in all his labor, he had never really

felt right before, not selling those goddamned rubbers and raincoats. But if he could cross this five yards. Could that be it? So late. So near the end with nothing at all, years lost as were those thousands of miles.

He could still hear the Gorilla grunting, rocking, rolling, as he reached the gun at last, checked the safety instinctively, as when he had gone shooting long ago, and slowly turned over.

The Gorilla was still at it, Mrs. Twitty's fingers caught spasmodically in the fur of his neck. The Cowboy was playing with himself, telling the Gorilla to hurry up, that he wanted another go. The Spaceman's helmet was foggy again, and the Skeleton had a fresh cigarette, trying to light it from the glowing butt of the last.

Mr. Twitty's first shot took off the Skeleton's skull. What Mr. Twitty remembered in his brief afterwards was not the blood and bone fragments and tissue splashed against his parlor wall, but the tiny sparks, like a flurry of fireflies, which spiraled away and upward into the darkness as the two cigarettes were blasted to one side.

But he saw all that in much less than a fraction of a second, because he was already pulling the trigger again, his second shot catching the Cowboy right in the groin he was playing with. The Cowboy was knocked backward and down, but he fell, back against the wall in such a way that his hands, relatively unhurt, went on playing, rummaging in the cavern of red slush for a second or two.

The Spaceman saw it coming and had just time enough to try to choose something to throw at Mr. Twitty. But he was still trying to pick between a vase with a picture of Cape Kennedy on it and an ashtray made of nose-cone ceramic when the charge hit him squarely in the chest. He sat down immediately, and as Mr. Twitty watched, praying in another part of his mind that there was no plug in the gun, that it held either four or five shots instead of the legal three, the Spaceman's helmet began to fill with blood which coursed from his mouth as if it would never stop flowing. It bubbled over his mouth, over his nose, but as he fell over backward, Mr. Twitty was already up on his feet aiming at the Gorilla.

The Gorilla was finished now. He was on his feet too, backing up toward the door, all the hatred and fury and lust gone from his face, his manlike crotch wilted, small and flabby now. Have you ever seen a terrified Gorilla?

— Please, the Gorilla was saying in a high cracked voice almost like that of a young boy. — Please, mister, for God's sake . . .

— Whoever heard of a Gorilla saying please, Mr. Twitty said as he pulled the trigger.

The Gorilla vanished in a tornado of fur and pieces of what appeared to be gorilla-meat. Mr. Twitty frowned, because he knew he had not hit him cleanly, and he could hear the thing flopping on the floor of the foyer. Flopping and howling just like the animal he was. But Mr. Twitty felt fine. Really fine. Later, he thought, I'll feel real bad, but shit I do feel fine just now.

— His name was George, Mrs. Twitty was saying from the sofa. — George Grotz. He traveled in cosmetics, and I *did* go, Sweet Jesus, I *did* go . . .

Mr. Twitty walked over to her, the sawed-off shotgun still fine and full in his hands. He looked down at her where she lay, naked, bleeding, exhausted, something like a lunatic smile on her bruised lips, kissed by so many things.

— Went where, Mr. Twitty asked her.

Mrs. Twitty opened her eyes and smiled up at him. — . . . me to know and you to find out, she whispered, and then drifted off.

Mr. Twitty could still hear that thing flopping in the foyer, and he intended to do something more, use that shotgun just once more, but he couldn't get it together, and before he could sort out some very strange impulses, the blood-high he was on faded and passed out. The last thing he heard was Mrs. Twitty flopping and that dying ape cooing — ... George, George ...

When the police came, they took one look and beat Mr. Twitty back into consciousness. One of them went around taking off masks, identifying the things Mr. Twitty had disposed of. He kept giving them the names of human beings, and sobbing as if his heart would break. While they waited for ambulances, they checked the brownies for hash. They sniffed the candied apples for Lysurgic acid. They examined the candy for signs of broken razor-blades or ground glass. They broke up several of the toys to find out if they contained explosives. One young detective who could not control himself kept cuffing Mr. Twitty every time he tried to tell what had happened, until an old detective told him to watch it, that the shriveled-up old scumbug was supposed to have some civil rights.

They paid no attention to Mrs. Twitty at all until one of the detectives noted that the soft-cushions weren't really red, and that possibly she was too mutilated to just be out on whiskey or dope after all.

A newspaper reporter came in, saw everything and vomited in the corner all over the rubble of Mrs. Twitty's glass animals. Then he pulled himself together and looked through the personal effects of the Cowboy and the Skeleton, the Spaceman and the Gorilla. It turned out that they had all belonged to prominent Belle Isle families, although Mr. Twitty, still fuddled, couldn't understand that at all.

They booked Mr. Twitty for what the junior assistant district attorney called Murder One, and tossed him into the county jail's bullpen with drunks, dope fiends, car thieves, draft dodgers, muggers, lily shakers and other perverts. When word got around that Mr. Twitty had butchered four young boys in cold blood, the drunks and muggers turned on him and beat him senseless. One of the perverts scratched him with its long fingernails and a dope fiend, still riding speed or strung out after acid, climbed up the iron bars of the bull pen and screamed insane things at him even after he couldn't hear any more.

Mrs. Twitty died in the hospital from internal injuries and hemorrhaging that night, but Mr. Twitty never heard about that, either, because he was in a coma when the guard came next morning to take him to his arraignment, and by late afternoon he died without making a statement. Death was attributed to his having fallen down in the bullpen, and it was hinted by a spokesman for the district attorney's office that perhaps narcotics was involved.

So Mr. and Mrs. Twitty never saw the newspaper articles about their bestiality or about the vast outpouring of public sentiment at the funerals of the Gorilla and the Cowboy and the Skeleton and the Spaceman. They had all gone to the same high school, and an editorial said that rarely had an American community being so tragically bereaved. The editorial also pointed up a moral in it all: something about how the jealousy of the past blighted the chances of the future. Some people wrote in, agreeing with that editorial, and one old maiden lady wrote saying things were not quite so simple. But nobody bothered to answer her, and that was the end of that.

The
Southern
Reporter

I

It was late in the afternoon when Judge Lambert took a
break. It was after a particularly bad clash between Caswell,
the prosecutor, and Tony Vallee, the defense attorney.
Judge Lambert, an old-timer who had sat on the First Judicial District Court in Shreveport since 1936, who had grown
old and even mild on the bench, told Caswell and Vallee
that one more such encounter would interrupt the trial—
while both counsel served a day or two in the Caddo Parish
Courthouse jail.

— With time enough to contemplate the monument down
below, dedicated to the memory of the Confederate Soldier,
who did his duty and held his tongue.

Dewey Domingue shook his head, spun his stenotype
around, and walked out of the courtroom, down the length
of the long antiseptic courthouse hall toward the coffee
machine. He put his quarter in and watched while the plastic
cup filled. A long time ago, Mrs. Mitchell, the deputy clerk,
had kept a pot of dark brew cut with chicory on a hot
plate in the clerk's office. The coffee had been good then,
the way it should be. The way Louisiana coffee always was.
But she had died in 1951, and her replacement had moved
out the coffeepot and had a machine put in.

Dewey stood drinking the thin, tasteless stuff, watching
witnesses, attorneys, parties to suits walking up and down
the hall. He had seen it all already. Seen them and their

141

antecedents walking up and down, stopping to talk in twos or threes, standing alone, smoking, leaning against the wall, staring into the late afternoon sun blankly, as if the stench of cigar smoke and snuff which no deodorant could purge from the hall had tranced them all.

In the First Judicial Court in Shreveport, both civil and criminal matters were heard. A reporter never knew what he might draw. One day, it was a suit on an open account. The next day it might be an axe murder or a mother who had decided to toss her children down an incinerator. Sometimes Dewey couldn't believe the words that flowed out from under his hands onto the tape. There were times when, staring down at the testimony, he could not believe those words had passed through his fingers. Sometimes, especially lately, he got the words wrong because he didn't even know what they meant.

Q. What did you do then?
A. Well uh you know like it was. Me or him so, you know, I cut him. I had this here sticker an he run at me an I uh stuck him on along his . . . gulley. He dropped an uh I tried to catch the Horse an an uh it was maybe fifty sixty bags uncut and uh uh he come up again an he tried to off me an uh you uh know uh . . .

Gibberish. And yet every time, no matter what they had done, there was always an appeal. Always the translation of those cryptic tapes into human language. Murray did that. He was Dewey's typist. Had been since 1949. Before that, he had been in the army. Murray couldn't remember how he had learned to type, or so he had once told Dewey. Only that he had learned when he found out in 1941 that if you could use a typing machine, they didn't put you in a rifle company. It had been a natural response for Murray. Yet now he was ashamed of it. When he drank a lot, he would tell Dewey that by rights he ought to be lying dead in the surf of some stinking Pacific atoll or long mouldering under the soil of France or Germany.

— One day I hadn't never seen no damned typewriter. The next week I was doing sixty words a minute. Now that's a natural-born coward for you. And if it had took a hundred and twenty, I'm mortally sure I could of done it. Ain't that a shame? Can't hardly spell his name till the hard rain starts to falling. Then all of a sudden he's a miracle worker, huh?

— I never knew anybody worked to get himself in a situation where he was bound to die, Dewey had told Murray early on. — Hell, I would have got to be a great cook, but I couldn't boil me an egg without I messed up the yolk. Don't fret about them days. Man can't spend his life looking backward, can he?

— Well, but I do, Murray said, and drank some more, and then went home out to Dixie Gardens where he had some kind of run-down old home and a wife. He had never asked Dewey out to his house, not in almost thirty years of working together, and Dewey never pried into anything, never asked any questions. You didn't go to prying when you worked with a man and he did his job. Dewey had learned that a long time ago. You take Murray. All he was was a typist, but he always came to court. Said he could do a better job of transcribing when he'd heard it all for himself. Dewey reckoned he was still down there in the courtroom waiting for it all to begin again. Murray never drank coffee. He drank beer and an awful amount of hard liquor. But he never missed an assignment, was never late. What else can you ask?

Dewey finished his coffee, crushed the flimsy cup contemptuously in his hand, and tossed it into a wastebasket lined with a plastic sack of some kind. Let me tell you what you can do with your damned machine coffee and your plastic garbage sacks, Dewey was thinking when Hilda came by.

Hilda was old. She was older than the present courthouse. She had worked for the First Judicial Court since when nobody could remember. She cleaned up the courthouse, the clerks' and judges' offices. She was old and black and angry and everybody made room for her and nobody gave her any trouble. Hilda paid no attention to you until you had been around the courts for twenty years or so. She was not about to clutter up her memory with names and faces and particulars of fly-by-night people. Enough trouble to keep straight the ones who mattered, the ones who were there all the time. She remembered as if it were yesterday the stir when Huey Long was elected governor. Caddo Parish had gone against him, but Hilda swore she had paid her poll tax and voted for Huey. He was a North Louisiana boy, a Protestant, and had no use for New Orleans. What more could you ask? They said he was a socialist. But what would he do about a parish in his own stomping ground that went against him?

— Didn't do a damned thing, Hilda would recount, her black face seamed with a repetition of laughter fifty years from its first expression. — Didn't do nothing bad. Didn't do nothing. No road repairs, no hep for the schools. Lissen, Old Huey lef 'em alone . . . Strickly alone. Never did 'em nothing. An they jus couldn't get up to faultin him. Them was quiet years, don't you know?

— What you say, Hilda asked Dewey.

— Can't say it, Momee, he answered. If you were an old timer, you called Hilda Momee. Nobody new had ever tried it. — How about you?

— I hear youall got a rape trial in there, she said.

— Not yet, Dewey smiled. — All the criminal assault I heard about so far is what them lawyers has been doing to each other.

Hilda didn't smile back. She stuck her mop in the wheeled bucket and took out her pack of Camels.

— It's a bad one, she said. — Girl name of Miranda Ferriday come up from Coushatta and got her a job over to Jumbo's Bar in Bossier City. Nice girl. Lookin to go to Meadows-Draughn Business. Had some typin and shorthand from Coushatta High. Fella name of Santidy started comin in, sniffin round her. She cute, an Jumbo make 'em wear them cut-off dresses, see? One night he took her out. Hardly got clear of the bar when he went after her. Poor thing never had a chance. Santidy a big man. Come from out west somewhere, I don't know. He did it, though. He did it, and that's sure.

The essence of a courthouse is the play of stories that moves within it. In the clerk's office, the civil sheriff's office, between the judges' clerks, between lawyers, between the women who clean up the courtrooms and the blind man who sells sandwiches and magazines in the lobby, there is a constant current of telling and hearing, of guessing and supposing as to the cases that are being acted out before the bench. The stories have no necessary connection with what will enter the records of each case. The rules of evidence do not constrain clerks and custodians, deliverymen and lawyers outside the purlieus of the court. What passes in the hallways of the courthouse may be strange, inaccurate, tainted with the passions of the storyteller. Still it may be nearer the truth than those pages that will be read by the court of appeal.

— That's sure, Hilda said again. — Santidy done it, and that poor girl fit him, see? She done tried to keep him off her, keep him away, but he wasn't havin none of that. He meant to git what he went for, see? An he did. Yes, he got it. I say jus lucky they cotch him.

— Who got him? Dewey asked, now for the first time interested in the case, intrigued. He put much faith in

Hilda's version of things. Over the years, had there been a morning line on the result of trials, and had he bet Hilda's insights, he would have been a wealthy man. She knew.

— Well, the police got him. What you think? Happens that poor girl's brother a police. Come up out of Coushatta a while back. What? Maybe two years. Got him a job with the Benton Sheriff's Office. Little girl live with him, see? An this Santidy goin to rape her out in front of the house, not even knowin her brother a police an him in the very house right then. Ain't that a shame?

— Well, if that's so, I reckon it is, Dewey said.

— What you mean if that's so?

— I reckon I mean, a lot of women claim . . .

Hilda looked disgusted. — You bet. Lots do. An a good number be lyin. But not this one, see?

Hilda drew on her Camel cigarette, leaned back against the wall. Her eyes, old and filmed, seemed softer than Dewey could remember. He paid a great deal of attention to the old woman. They were friends, contemporaries. They knew what few others knew.

— You know, Hilda said almost nostalgically. — I can remember when a man did that to a woman was a good as dead . . . Never got to trial . . .

— But . . . Wasn't it mostly . . . ?

— Nigger men? Sure enough. When they took 'em out, I used to say, shame. That's an awful thing . . .

Hilda mashed out her cigarette on the sole of her shoe.

— Sure, that's what I used to say. But now is now. An I know what's goin down just as well as anybody. An I tell you this: was they to go to lynchin again, an be fair . . . Take 'em all out that did what that damn Santidy did, never mind no color . . . you know what?

— What?

— I wouldn't say shame. I wouldn't say one damn thing but good enough for 'em.

Dewey was surprised. — That's hard, he said. — Now, Momee . . .

— Don't Momee me, boy. I'm an old woman, an I see what we got goin nowadays. You know what we come to? No Jesus. That's what we got. You turn away from Jesus, what you expect?

— Not much, Dewey said. — No, I wouldn't expect too much.

— You ain't got no Jesus, your ass in a sling, see?

— I believe so, Dewey said soberly. And he did. That was what he believed. He had believed it for a long time.

Dewey Domingue had come up from the Florida Parishes to Shreveport in 1939. He had worked in Hammond on the railroad and out of Madisonville crabbing and had, before he was twenty, gone into New Orleans against the advice of all his people, hoping to better himself. He had a strong clean handwriting taught him by his mother, and he had come to spell English words tolerably on his own. He was not ashamed of his French, but he wanted to go forward in the world, and you didn't go forward using Cajun French. No, what you did was learn that English that the big people, the important people used. So he had gotten himself a job in the New Orleans Civil District Courts. He had learned shorthand after awhile. They paid good money. But God knows he had not bettered himself. It was just as his people had said. New Orleans was a terrible town, and no decent young man could sustain himself there. Not for long. He had lost his faith in New Orleans. He had consorted with whores and men who lived off them. He had taken to the night life. Lord, the things he had seen. Women shameless and forlorn, stripping off their clothes, offering themselves on table tops and long oaken bars. Drunkenness and gambling. Even sodomy. If there was a filth in the world that had not found its way to New Orleans, Dewey did not know its name. Except for one drunken Sunday afternoon when he had accidentally stumbled into Saint Louis Cathedral behind a pack of gawking tourists, he had not been to mass since he left the parishes. Was that bettering himself?

Looking backward, Dewey could remember those days as if they were disconnected scenes from an old movie. He remembered working the courts during the day, his mind already on sundown, on the Quarter. He remembered the heat that would rise within him, the fantasies that played across the ragged unfinished stage of his mind as he sat writing, amanuensis with the panoply and color and tension of Saint Anthony's temptations firing his hopes for evening.

At last, more to assure himself those evenings than for any other reason, he had set up housekeeping with a girl from Baton Rouge no wiser than he. It had been the strangest game: the two of them putting aside whatever they had been before they came to New Orleans, wordlessly pretending that this was their place, this the form of their lives.

Each night they would go from one steamy club to the next. The one run by a woman, gross and overweight, who nestled an enormous ruby between her vast breasts and smiled off questions, saying that the blood-red stone was the price her virtue had brought so long before when things were really good, before the Navy had put everyone out on the street. Or the one run by a man from New York who had once piloted the China Clipper till the liquor took him, and he found himself in the bowels of Shanghai when it was the sewer of the world. They would drink and sing and dance until they were exhausted with the world. Then they would go back to their tiny one-room apartment on Royal Street, turn on the oscillating fan and make what passed for love between them until dawn. Time for him to go to court. Time for her to go to the oyster bar and wash and clean till opening time.

He had known something was wrong. Not the sin or the shame of it, not simply the commonness, the trashiness of living that way. It had gone deeper.

It would be years later before he would find the words to say, even to himself, what had really been wrong with it. It was that, growing up in the parishes, somewhere, somehow, he had come to expect more. Was what he felt for the girl (named Viola, for all it mattered then or later; from Clinton, not Baton Rouge, for all anyone cared at the time or afterward) all there was to feel? Was it some flaw in him or in her? In both of them or in the world? They had met and hungered and said it was fine to eat when you are hungry, isn't it? Who makes promises to gumbo or fried trout? Being free is doing what you want to do, isn't it? Sure, Dewey had told her, a little less certainly than the question had been asked—but just as sure he wanted to be free.

Freedom wasn't a place or a thing, but what it seemed to be was a golden glow suffusing whatever else the idea of it touched. They were free. New Orleans was free. This life was what it was to be free. Wasn't it? Sure, Dewey told himself. I can say what I want, do what I want. Can't I?

Still there existed the shadow he could hardly trace through the days and nights, some faintest sour residuum that only forced its way into consciousness when he was exhausted during a trial recess or very early in the morning as he strode out under the faded parchment of the sky in the dark streets before dawn.

Then there had been that afternoon in August when it had been too hot to go on, when the judge had recessed court on account of the ungodly heat, saying they would reconvene at seven in the evening and go forward in that way until the heat wave broke. Dewey had been upset, irritated that he would have to lose a night on the town, walking and talking, drinking and dancing with his woman, sitting with the sports and musicians in the clubs, listening to the pulse of real life as it drummed in the streets after dark.

When he reached the apartment, he heard sounds inside. The heat was awful, enough to make his head swim. Maybe the sounds were from next door. Maybe he ought to go down to the A & P and pick up a dozen bottles of beer. Maybe he should go by the oyster bar. He shut his eyes, key in hand, defeated, broken already, with nothing fine and free to do or say, nothing at all left but to practice the tiny heroism of turning the key in his own door and walking into the future he already knew lay spread in the stark heat of midday there.

All she had said, almost dreamily, was — Oh, shit, Dewey, what are you doing home so early?

Later, sitting with his fifth double bourbon in hand, he would remember it as if it had been etched in the contours of his brain so that another angle, another view would confront him no matter what direction he might choose to push his thought. The fact was not so awful as the encounter, the reality of it being stamped in his memory past remove, past casting out or burying or even attempting to forget.

Later, sitting there, he thought he had not loved her, could never have loved her. But if that was so, then where did the pain come from? Was it just the instantaneous sight of that pale, naked, hairy body he had glimpsed for less than a moment moving rhythmically, absurdly, over her? Was it some diminution of his own manhood that had called inexorably for violence he had not even thought of at that moment?

No. He had not loved her. But she had been what he had voluntarily put in the place of love. He had made himself a life full of substitutions, hadn't he? Surely he had. He had burned himself out so thoroughly that whatever there might have been in life beyond was now barred to him forever. Not by law or creed or opinion, but by his own loss of feeling, that horror and cynicism now as much a part of him as his eyes, his ears—his memories.

He had drunk then. For a brief while, he had managed to hold on to his job at the Civil District Courts, but finally that had gone, the judicial administrator angrily firing him when it was found that the stenographic transcript for a whole trial was a hopeless muddle, which even Dewey himself could not interpret.

After that, he had taken to drinking cheap wine and sitting in Lafayette Park in the afternoons as autumn came on. He talked to the men who came there, and they told him that life made no sense at all, that it was good to watch dogs seeking lampposts or fire hydrants, and to listen to music when one could. But that life made no sense at all.

He did odd jobs for people who had known him in better days. When there were no jobs, there was the Salvation Army with good rich soup, a dry corner in a deserted warehouse where amidst the cooling nights he could hear the distant, hopeless foghorns of ships entering and leaving the port, sounding as if they were mourning a home they would never reach, perhaps one they could not even recall.

It was deep winter when his string played out. He awoke to find himself lying on the grass at the base of the Lee Monument, his eyes suddenly open, staring up toward the chill sky, and finding there the image of Robert E. Lee, arms crossed, hat pulled over his eyes, staring north where the enemy lay, where it had always been. The next thing he remembered was a young resident at Charity Hospital telling him that the Huey P. Long Bridge was a better and easier way to go than what he was doing to himself.

And after that, he remembered being on the street outside the hospital, walking along Tulane Avenue back toward downtown, where everything had happened to him. The Huey P. Long Bridge lay behind him. Perhaps there was an inch or two left to his string. As he walked, he found he had no feelings at all—but still there was an awful thirst.

Then, almost to Canal Street, at the verge of the Quarter, he had seen an ancient truck from which men were selling produce: oranges, strawberries, tomatoes, cushaws. There were two of them, and they were speaking French, and Yes, of course they would share their lunch with him. How had he come to live in this place? No, of course they didn't. No, they came here only to sell what they grew. This was not place for a decent man to live. Hadn't his priest told him about this place? Yes, Dewey lied. Of course he had. One more question: Would there be a little work for a man who wanted to . . . walk away?

Afterward, when he was himself again, or at least some self that could work and sleep and leave the liquor alone, he had considered going home. Bastien and Robert, his truck-farming friends said that was the thing to do. Home. Or west to Evangeline Parish where even now people lived life the way it was meant to be lived.

No, Dewey thought. At least not yet. There has got to be something else that has to be done. Maybe feelings can be rescued, found again, but not home. Not with a family or normal people watching, wondering what has gone wrong inside their kinsman. Better another place. Surely better a place where one is . . . What? Free?

Then he had found himself a map of Louisiana one Sunday afternoon, and looked it over. After considering for the length of that long dreary Sunday afternoon, he had packed his things, gone to the bus depot, and bought a ticket for Shreveport, the farthest place he had any knowledge of. He had heard of Texas and Mississippi. He knew there were such places as Arkansas, New York, and France, but those places had no more real existence for Dewey than did

Samarkand or Tycho or the Asteroid Belt. Not in 1939.

So he had gone to Shreveport and found himself a job
there in the courts. Lord knows he had tried hard to live a
good life. And it had turned out to be easy. There was
no Bourbon Street there, no steady, inescapable invition to
sin, no depravity so general and sustained that a man could
not avoid it if he walked out into the open streets. All a
man had to do was mind his business. There was Bossier
City, surely. But that was across the river, and he did not go
there. Had no call to go there. He did his work and went
home and listened to the radio and read the Shreveport
Times. On weekends, he would ride out to Ford Park and
walk under the tall pines, or go to the public pier on Cross
Lake and hire a boat and fish. He would bring a box of
worms and fish from before daylight until after dark, often
taking home a mess of bream and small cat. Since he had
no place to keep them, he always gave them to Murray.
Years earlier, he had hoped—perhaps even expected—that
Murray would ask him out to Dixie Gardens to share the
fish, fried in cornmeal with hush puppies, french fries, and
a little salad. But that had not happened, and after a few
years, Dewey had stopped expecting that it might. Still he
went on handing the fish he caught over to Murray as if
they were in some way an established tribute in kind,
something he owed.

He snapped out of his remembering in time to see Hilda
limping off, pushing her mop and bucket before her. She
turned back, fixed Dewey with her eyes. — You gonna see.
That Santidy guilty as sin, you hear?

— Well, Dewey said, and Hilda disappeared around a
corner. But now Dewey was interested. All there had been
so far was Vallee the defense against Caswell the prosecutor.
Rhetoric against rhetoric. But if Hilda was right, as she
usually was, then maybe he should pay attention. Usually
he didn't. Nothing was at issue but somebody's time, some-

body's money. It was funny how everything got reduced to that in court. Somebody was going to serve time or he wasn't. Somebody was going to have to pay money or he wasn't. But Hilda didn't care about that. She never had anything to say about a case unless there was more at issue. Dewey would pay attention now.

Murray came out of the courtroom, wiping his forehead. He almost always came to the trials. He would joke and say he had to be at the trials to make out Dewey's transcript, but they both knew better. Dewey was the best they had at the stenotype in the First Judicial Court. No, Murray came whenever he didn't have a transcript to type up because he loved the courts. Dewey understood that. Murray had been hurt in the war. He had lost a leg sitting in a headquarters company office. A shell had come in and killed almost everyone in the office. Somehow, Murray had survived. He should have been proud, Dewey reasoned. How many clerk-typists had been awarded the Purple Heart? But somehow that shell had made Murray ashamed. Now, even though bereft of his leg, he seemed to live in a world of his own, wishing that leg had been lost in some better venture. He had once told Dewey that lesser men had been injured in the Battle of Bulge or the crossing of the Remagen bridge. Others had lost much less lying amidst the ruin of their own flesh, staring across the Rhine toward the smoking distant bank, like Moses at Pisgah, seeing with sadness and relief a shore they would never reach. To lose so much sitting behind a typewriter, typing the company sick list was a terrible thing, Murray would say.

— Judge is ready, Murray said.

They began again. Vallee's objections served as punctuations to the testimony. Police officer who had been called. Her brother, her boss at Jumbo's. Then Caswell, the assistant district attorney, called Miranda to the stand. Dewey wached her walk toward the witness stand.

She was small, with dark eyes and long jet-black hair and smooth olive skin. Dewey watched her, his eyes following as she walked to the stand, eyes down, and seated herself in a silence drawn around her like a shawl.

Miranda Ferriday did not look like a North Louisiana girl to Dewey. He remembered such girls in the bayou country, in Hammond, in New Orleans. He was drawn to her. Dewey did not care for the washed-out blonds and dull brown-haired girls with freckles and pale skin who peopled the upper parishes. But then he had not much thought of girls since he had left New Orleans for the shame of those days. This girl was different. As she was sworn, Dewey could see the two of them, him and her, together. Lord, how long had it been since he had had such feelings? Twenty years? No, more nearly thirty. It didn't matter. As Miranda sat waiting for Caswell to begin his questions, Dewey's fingers poised above the stenotype. From somewhere inside him there arose that power and horror that he almost forgot he possessed merely by being a man. He was astonished at himself. The old Adam might lie silent for twenty years or more and yet not be slain. But then Caswell began, and Dewey's fingers followed him.

Caswell was gentle, considerate. He was a large man, coarse and overweight, his shirt collar pressing into his neck. But it seemed that he knew how awful Miranda's experience had been, how difficult it was for her to recall it, to testify about it before the court and the jury. Still, in order that justice be done, and that others might not suffer as she had, she realized the importance of her testimony. Isn't that so? Caswell asked. Miranda looked up at him and nodded slowly, her expression suddenly intense, her eyes watchful.

She told of her home down in Coushatta. Her father had owned a filling station until he came down with consumption and had been sent to the Pines T.B. Sanatorium. Her mother had died in a house fire, and she had come to Shreveport to be with her brother, a deputy sheriff in Benton, Louisiana, Bossier Parish.

Miranda admitted that she did not like the work at Jumbo's. But Mr. Jumbo was nice to her. He was himself a retired policeman, a friend of her brother's. Anyhow, you had to have work. Nobody in her family didn't work. Everyone was supposed to work, weren't they?

Yes, she had met one Santidy there. He had come from the west. He said California. Is there a Bakersville? Bakersfield? All right, yes, I reckon. And he would come in most especially on Monday and Friday evenings, usually late. He liked funny drinks. Sidecars, grasshoppers, screwdrivers, manhattans. He was tall and dark and always laughing. He noticed her. He talked to her. He took to leaving her five-dollar tips. He liked to buy drinks for everybody in the place and to have people notice him. He worked up at Oil City, sometimes in East Texas: Kilgore, Longview, Tyler, Gladewater, Marshall. It was his job to strip old wells. He was one who knew how to get the last drop out of wells nearly empty. There was good money in it. He used to laugh and ask Miranda if she was a stripper, too. She would blush and ignore him then.

As Miranda went on, interrupted by Caswell's questions, Dewey let her voice carry him back to the long cuts and bayous around Lake Ferdinand, south of New Orleans. He remembered trips with his father to those places, austere, the banks and shores covered with harsh brush and palmetto. His hands worked automatically, putting down the words she said. He could close his eyes remembering and go on typing, listening and recording without hearing or caring. Still, he did care, and he could not tell just why. He wished he could take a break now. He needed to go outside.

On a certain night, Miranda said, Santidy had come in. He was flush with money, buying round after round of drinks, people applauding when someone behind the bar would, for a moment, cut off the jukebox and tell who had bought the drinks for the house. The people at the tables, along the bar had come to know Santidy and appreciate him. He drank and she served. It came near closing time. He asked if she had a way home. She said, No, no she didn't. He laughed and touched her, saying, Let me take you home, honey. You know it's dark and a long, long night. At first she ignored him. But after all he was very popular. Somehow she supposed that someone so well known, so much thought of in the place, would be trustworthy. At the very least for the distance between Jumbo's bar and her brother's home.

But it had not turned out that way. No, rather he had taken her in his car, driven away from Jumbo's, gone this way and that, twisting up one street and down another until her head had begun to spin. Then, somewhere along the levee, he had stopped the car, turned to her and told her in the most obscene terms what he expected, demanded of her. She had almost fainted, but before she could, he was upon her.

The rest of it was difficult to follow, the outpouring of one who could hardly remember coherently what she had to tell. What had happened to her? Dewey listened to it all. His fingers moved, independent of what went on, but still he heard.

Santidy had brought her home, sure enough. He had stopped his car out in front of her brother's house, where he had said terrible things to her, where he had taken her again, done what he wanted to do with her. She had fought against him, had cried out, had wept and pled with him. But none of it had mattered.

And when he had done with her, he had laughed once more, opened the car door, and pushed her into the street. Like garbage. And driven away.

Caswell patted his brow with a folded handkerchief and sat down. — Thank you, Miss Ferriday, he said. — That's all I have.

There was a moment's pause then. Dewey relaxed, thinking, Hilda was right. Now that's the way it was. Then Vallee stood up for cross. Dewey hoped Judge Lambert might call for a recess. But the judge looked at Vallee and said nothing. Dewey spaced his tape and waited.

At first Vallee was as quiet, as gentle as Caswell had been. He asked Miranda about her past down in the country, asked about her home life, about her religious education, asked if she had had boy friends back then. Miranda answered openly, like one without guilt. But then the questioning closed in, became more personal. Vallee began stalking her life a wolf, moving question by question from counsel's table toward the witness stand until he enclosed it, his arms almost around it as he pressed one question after another. Dewey didn't like his method. It was almost as if he were embracing her, drawing her close, as if his questions were intimate rather than public. He wanted to know about her sexual experience as a young girl. He wanted to know about her lovers, and he was so close to her, it was as if he deemed himself her next friend rather than an attorney doing what was expected, demanded of him. Vallee wanted to know why she had chosen Jumbo's as a place to work. Surely she had known that Jumbo's was a swinging place, a place where the live crowd came. Hadn't she picked Jumbo's for that very reason? Hadn't she come up from the parishes looking for action? Wanting excitement? Wasn't that the way it was?

Dewey made a record, listening and typing. Yet still he heard. Surely no one saw him shudder as Vallee pressed on, his voice soft and insinuating. He had heard so many of them, Dewey had. Lawyers who could somehow alter reality to suit their cause. It was like listening to the serpent arguing with Eve. Only Eve hadn't been to law school as the serpent surely had.

Q. Now Miss Ferriday, you're a grown woman, aren't you?
A. Yes. Sure. I guess so.
Q. Well then, if a man approaches you . . .
A. . . . Approaches me . . . What do you mean . . . approaches?
Q. Come now, Miss Ferriday. I mean a man who approaches a woman . . . as a man . . . approaches a woman.
Mr. Caswell. Objection, Your Honor.
The Court. Yes, Mr. Caswell . . . ?
Mr. Caswell. I suggest, even in these times, a man may approach a woman with something other than rape in mind . . .
Mr. Vallee. May it please the Court, I'm sure I haven't suggested anything like that in my questioning. . . . May counsel approach the bench?
Mr. Caswell. Indeed, your honor. Since approaching seems to be the essence of counsel's questioning . . .

The lawyers went up to the bench before Judge Lambert, and Dewey relaxed for a moment. There was a nice irony in the fact that when the lawyers reached the very peak of their concern, moving to the bench to argue a point of law, the reporter could relax, because their argument, however intense, was not recorded. Dewey closed his eyes and let all his faculties ease off. Part of being a court reporter was responding to the court, knowing when to catch every word, and knowing when to relax.

Over his shoulder, he heard the cut and slash of argumentation passing between Caswell and Vallee. But he also knew who would prevail. In a close matter, the defense always prevailed. Judge Lambert would have it otherwise, but he did not want to be reversed. That would most likely call for another trial. Judge Lambert did not want another trial. He was old now and tired. If he could, he would mete out the death sentence for rape on a prima facie case. But that was not possible. Not with the weight of federal courts above seemingly committed to the proposition that every criminal defendant was a prince, about to be victimized by the prosecution. So Dewey rested, knowing that when they went back on the record, it would be Vallee's question. That was how the game played.

Sure enough, when the conference at the bench was done, Vallee asked his question again.

Q. Miss Ferriday, let me ask you again, when Mr. Santidy asked you out...asked you to leave Jumbo's with him...
A. Yes...
Q. I mean...You knew what he had in mind, now didn't you?
A. ...In mind...I don't...what...
Q. Come now. You're not a child . . .
A. No...that's...
Q. You knew where it was leading, now didn't you?

There was a sudden silence, and Dewey's head turned around to see her. She sat in the witness box helpless, trying to find words to tell the truth.

A. No. I mean, I never thought...
Q. Come now, Miss Ferriday, you've worked at Jumbo's quite a while, haven't you? When a man asks you out...
A. No, listen...I try to be...
Q. When you go out, it's just for a drink and a quick trip home, right?
A. Yes. Listen, I never . . .
Q. Right. You never. That's why you choose to work at one of the roughest lounges in Bossier City...
Mr. Caswell: Objection. I ask that counsel's last remarks be stricken. No foundation has been laid to suggest that . . .

It was almost dark now. They had broken for dinner. Dewey had picked up a chicken salad sandwich down in the lobby before the blind man shut up for the day. He had gotten a half-pint of milk, too. Now he sat in the back bench of the courtroom, eating slowly. Murray limped up and sat beside him.

— Shit, I'm tired. Ain't you?

— You know it, Dewey said.

— It's a goddamned shame, Murray said. — I mean having to go through this crap.

— Huh?

— I mean, you know that lousy bastard did it. He raped her...

— Well ... Yes, I reckon ... I mean ...

— Aw, come on, Dewey. You better believe it. I mean, that little girl thought she had a ride home, and he pulled her down ...

Dewey chewed for a long time. Then he swallowed and washed it down with some milk. — I just can't hardly believe a man would do that to a young girl. I mean ... even today ...

Murray snorted, and a rill of coffee ran down his chin. — I be goddamned if I ever will understand you, Dewey. I mean you live in the same world with the rest of us. You read about that whore in Chicago who wanted to go to a party and couldn't find no baby-sitter for her six-months-old baby girl? Huh? Yeah, well, it was in the *Journal*. What she did? Well, she threw the baby down a trash incinerator. From the sixth floor. Yeah, well, that's today for you. This world is a shit heap. I mean, that greasy-looking bastard Santidy, he done just what Caswell makes out that he did. I wisht they'd just let me have him. Boy, you just give me five minutes alone with him ... Us veterans know how to handle 'em ...

Then Murray stood up slowly and limped back and forth in front of the judge's bench saying what he would do to Santidy if they let him have the motherless son of a bitch. It was bad, what he said, and Dewey almost gagged on his sandwich. While Murray limped and fulminated, Caswell the prosecutor came in. He stood back and listened for a minute or two. Then he told Murray he wished to hell he had him on the jury.

— That greaseball is going to walk, Caswell said, staring at his fingernails.

— You think so, Dewey asked, surprised.

— Sure, Caswell said. — Easiest thing in the world. I don't know why we even try these things. Ought to take rape off the books. Maybe put it under assault with a deadly weapon.

Murray and Caswell laughed bitterly together. For a moment Dewey didn't understand.

— Everybody's a whore—except your own wife or mother or sister. That's the way these goddamn juries see it. I bet I've lost twenty cases like this if I've lost one.

— That's . . . terrible, Dewey said.

— Sure it's terrible, Caswell told him. — But that's the system, ol buddy. Can't diddle with the system, right?

Caswell was tired, Dewey could see that. He let his bulk settle into one of the chairs back of counsel's table. He was not an old man, rather a man of indecipherable age, probably in his forties. But his face was heavy, lined, wise—like the countenance of an elephant, full of scars and wrinkles. Dewey seemed to remember that Caswell had been local commander of the American Legion. — I've won a lot of 'em and lost a lot of 'em, you understand?

Caswell closed his eyes and leaned back in the chair he had chosen. — Lord God, I been every way you can be. We used to be able to put some of 'em in the chair. All you had to do was spring that girl on him. Let her tell folks what had happened.

Caswell opened his eyes, grinned slowly. — But that was when your old ordinary juror still believed there was such a thing as a nice girl. Seems like a long time ago.

— Makes you wonder, Murray said. — Maybe the system

don't work. I mean, what did we fight for? So some nasty bastard could come in here and do whatever the hell he wants. I mean, a girl like that . . . She *had* to work, and them places . . .

Caswell stared at the polished limestone behind the judge's bench. — Nothing in this shit-eating society works any more. The whole damned thing's coming unglued. You think this is a bad case? Hell, at least the girl's alive. He didn't push her eyes out. He didn't cut off her tits. I try capital cases. Murders like you wouldn't believe if I was to tell you. Absolute proof, and the goddamned jury hands 'em five years. Just time to get ready for the next one.

Caswell told them the circumstances and details of a recent case. Dewey and Murray looked at each other, sickened. Caswell laughed sardonically. — That's what you can do to a nine-year-old girl in Louisiana. And get twenty years. Parole maybe in seven.

— My God, Dewey said, numbed by what he had heard.

— Evidentiary rules, Caswell snorted. — That dirty piece of filth had three assaults on minors on his record. He'd been a time bomb waiting to go off. Could I show that? Hell, no. He hadn't been convicted. One thing and another, and they'd dropped the charges or let him plead to a lesser offense. They *knew* that bastard was gonna kill a child . . . And when he did, I couldn't tell the jury what he'd been pulled in for three times before . . .

— Maybe we're trying the wrong people, Murray said ominously.

— You want things to change? Caswell asked rhetorically. — I can give you formula. Let every last family in this country have a rape or a murder in it—not a robbery. That won't get it. It's got to be one of the big ones. Better it happen all on the same night . . .

— Like to Pharaoh and the Egyptians, Dewey put in.

— From the White House to the cropper's shack down

on the river. Then these damned beasts of burden would start handing out death sentences like prizes in Cracker Jack. Give me five, six hundred executions a year for ten or fifteen years. You'd be downright amazed how quiet things would get.

— Them as do wrong has got to pay the price, Murray said. — Everybody knows that.

— Bullshit, Caswell said easily. — Nobody knows no such damned thing. I tell you what. People kinda like to see a smooth operator get by with something. You look at that girl, Miranda. Putting law and decency aside, who wouldn't like to get her in a car, talk to her. Kiss her. So then she decides she's gone far enough, but your imagination is already a long way past a little kiss, so you kind of manhandle her a little. You pull off her blouse. None of that old high school fooling with buttons. This is the big time. You just grab it by the front and ... Ah, look there. Big fine boobs almost busting out of her brassiere. But that can wait, cause when you see what she's got, you go for the skirt. Get in between her legs with one hand, cover her mouth with the other. Lay on top of her. Don't let her get loose ... Oh, them long luscious legs ...

Dewey and Murray looked at one another, then back at Caswell, whose eyes glinted as he went on in more and more bald and intimate detail, describing what it must have been like to rape Miranda Ferriday, rape her right down into the ground. Dewey couldn't help being drawn along, reenacting in his own mind what Caswell was saying. It was awful, but in the recesses of his mind, Dewey could feel that old Adam pulling, clawing at the structure of his own control.

When Caswell finished, he was breathing rapidly, smiling, looking from Murray to Dewey and back again. — Now when you come right down to it, saving the law and decency, all that's worth a little risk, ain't it? I mean, just reckon you didn't know any better, or even knowing, didn't give a damn? Say you'd been raised in California. Hell of a way to pass an hour, huh?

Murray was blushing. Dewey stared at the floor.

— Shit, Murray said in an injured tone. — I thought you was against that kind of thing.

Caswell's expression of visionary pleasure vanished as if someone had shut a door in his heavy red face.

— I am, he said. — I sure as hell am. But I know what sin is. A man's got to know what sin is if he's gonna fight it. You see that, don't you?

— He hadn't ought to lust after the sin he's fighting, Dewey said quietly. — He ought not to know it all that well . . .

Caswell shrugged, heaved his bulk out of the chair, glanced at his watch. — You boys are nice. But you're shit kickers. You got it in for Santidy cause he cut that little girl. I got it in for him cause he broke the law. Reckon if he had spent a little time, talked her into a good screw right out in the car, telling her about love and the stars and how happiness was just a pant and a promise away? You'd still have it in for him. I wouldn't. That's good stuff, and a man needs it. But the law says you got to be polite. Mustn't grab. Got to ask. You got to have it *given* to you. Now a shit kicker sees sin as corruption and damnation. A lawyer sees it as disorder. It don't make a damn what's done, so long as it's done orderly. And orderly means law. Hell, I'd slap a child away from his own table for grabbing at the chicken on a platter. Same way with Santidy. I'd like to see him slapped right out of this world.

Caswell made a broad gesture. — Why, I don't give a damn if they legalize murder—so long as they set out rules, so everybody can know 'em.

Murray stared at him. — What if some woman was to throw her six-months-old baby down an incinerator chute? How about that?

Caswell narrowed his eyes. — We got a law against that.

Dewey hardly dared ask. — What if we didn't?

Caswell laughed, the sound rich and fluid, coming from deep within him. — Well, you couldn't get her for littering, could you?

— Jesus, Murray said and moved off.

Dewey licked his lips. There was something he wanted to say, but he wasn't sure he had the right. After all, he had sinned, had done terrible things even though a long time ago. Still, it seemed something had to be said.

— I . . . think . . .

Caswell smiled at him. — I bet you do, Dewey. You're always mighty quiet, but there's something going on with you, ain't there?

— I think it's got to be more . . . than just law.

Caswell frowned. — Now coming from an old-time court reporter, that's goddamned near treason. Hell, Dewey, if we ain't convinced you, I think we got trouble . . . Right here in River City . . .

He laughed, but Dewey didn't join in. Something was hurting him. As if there had been something lost, something he could not name or put into words. Something Caswell purposely slighted in his buffoon's performance about law and order. Dewey thought as hard as he could, his eyes squinted almost closed.

— It don't change a thing because you say it's legal. Even if you pass a law . . .

Caswell leaned down over Dewey, his large eyes shining with an almost maniacal certainty.

— I don't blame you. I honest to God don't. When I come up to Shreveport from down at Jena, I felt the same way. Hell, even before that, before I went to LSU Law School, I knew right from wrong better than any circuit judge in this chicken-shit state. My folks learned me good and evil. Reverend Trotter set 'em out clear as good water in a running stream. But . . . things don't go that way.

Caswell stood up, and moved away, his back to Dewey. Suddenly he turned, pointing his finger at Dewey as if court were in session, and Dewey the witness being examined.

— *You* know what's good and evil. *I* know what's right and wrong. But the courts don't. People don't. Lord God, the mind of man can conjure up wickedness that decent folks never even thought to prohibit. And that don't even take into consideration the mind of woman. Do justice, folks say . . . but not to me. Whatever I do is okay. Abortion, sodomy, adultery, rape . . . Whatever we learned was wrong as kids is just all right today. You got to put good and evil out of your mind, Dewey. You got to. Because they won't let us keep those words. They don't mean anything. What I can't figure is how you've held on to 'em so long. Don't you see what I mean? Forget good and evil. Think legal and illegal. Maybe we can make a stand there . . .

His voice trailed off, and Dewey could hear in it for the first time Caswell's pain, the sense of loss that was barely papered over by his cynicism. He walked back to the prosecutor's table and picked up a file. Dewey thought he could see tears in Caswell's eyes.

— You got to take the law and grab hold of it, and say: Law, be thou my good . . . Nonlaw, be thou my evil. Now you *got* to do that . . .

— No, Dewey heard himself say, his voice louder than he realized until he heard it. — Because law is supposed to come out of what's good. You can't make no kind of good out of law . . .

Caswell sat down again at the distant table, and Dewey could see now, sure enough, that tears were coursing down his cheeks, down that face that looked like a side of fresh-slaughtered beef. Caswell shook his head like an old bull pestered by a myriad of flies.

— Well, goddamn it, you got to. You ain't got any choice.

Because if you don't, it'll kill you. It'll break your heart.
You know what I mean?

— No.

— Hell, Dewey . . .

— I can't help it, Dewey said. Things don't get to be . . .
other things cause you put another name on 'em. You could
make laws all year. If they was wrong, they'd be wrong.
And a jury can't make wrong right.

— It'll break your heart thinking that way, Caswell told
him. — Look, I'm gonna be district attorney one day soon.
People like me, you know? After that, I could go to the
legislature . . . Hell, I could be governor. I could do that.
I got a lot of support out in the parishes.

— Well, Dewey said softly, — I reckon you could do all
that. But it wouldn't change nothing. Wouldn't make a
good man bad, or a bad man good . . .

Caswell rubbed his eyes, threw up his hands.

— I'm wasting my time, he said. — You ain't heard a goddamned thing I've said. Can't you see all that good/evil
stuff has gone by the board?

Dewey said nothing, and Caswell was quiet for a long
moment. — But I wish it hadn't. I wish, after this no-nut
jury lets Santidy go, I wish you and me and that crippled
feller . . . What's his name?

— Murray, Dewey said. — He ain't crippled. He's a war
veteran.

— Who ain't? I'd like to see the three of us go find that
greasy bastard and give him a little justice. Not law. Justice.

— That seems what folks ought to do, Dewey began.

— But we can't. Those old fools on the Supreme Court
says we can't, and all those New York Jew liberals. Mustn't
do. Naughty. Man who does that is *not* going to the legislature, right? Right. No, he's gonna pick up a few years for
violating that ugly bastard's civil rights. So all right. I understand. No justice. No damned justice. What we're doing

here folks is the law. We're gonna smile if we win and
smile if we lose. Cause that's how we all get along, ain't it,
Dewey?

— That's what you tell me.

— And it's gospel, ol buddy. You just sit there and do
your job, and see how this case comes out. See what happens.

Judge Lambert opened the door of his chambers and
signaled to his minute clerk who was almost asleep on the
last bench in the courtroom. He got up slowly to round up
Vallee and Santidy, and whatever witnesses might be left.
When he had them all lined up, he would bring out the
jury. Then it would all get started again. Dewey went back
to his stenotype and got ready. He did not look at Caswell.
It was hard to think about all he'd said.

The rest of the prosecution's case wasn't much. Yes, the
coroner said, there was evidence of recent sexual intercourse
when he examined Miranda. Yes, there were bruises and
minor abrasions. Yes, they were consistent with an assault.
No, they did not prove assault. And so on. Yes, the investi-
gating officer said, when Santidy was arrested, there were
scratches. Small ones on his hands and face. But . . . yes?
Vallee asked, Weren't there others? Large ones, the officer
said. Down his back.

Vallee spun toward the jury, his eyes gleaming as if he
and they shared knowledge of a certain filthy joke between
them.

— Where?

— Down his back, around his shoulders.

— That's all, Vallee smiled, pleased, already opening another witness folder.

When the State's case had finally wound down to its
conclusion, Vallee smiled again, and called his only witness.
It was Santidy.

Santidy had been sitting, almost slouching in his chair

throughout the trial, like some somnolent animal, sleepy and well fed, only marginally aware of what was passing around him, unconcerned that somehow it all had to do with him. Dewey had watched him off and on, especially while Miranda was testifying. As she answered Caswell's questions, he would turn and shake his head, grin at Vallee, who would smile back and shake his head as if the two of them, firm in the truth of Santidy's innocence, could only look with bemused indulgence on Miranda's pathetic, hysterical lies.

Santidy rose then, seemed to stretch a little as he walked to the witness stand with measured insouciance. Dewey glanced around and saw Murray's jaw tighten as Santidy was sworn.

Then Santidy sat down in the witness chair, a mild, benevolent smile on his lips. He was tall, well built, with broad shoulders and narrow hips, much like one of those male models who show off expensive clothes for department stores and clothiers. He seemed composed, uninvolved, as if he were at most a witness rather than a defendant. He had a thick bush of silky hair with enormous sideburns, a gold diamond ring on his left little finger, and he wore a tight, close-fitting body shirt open at the collar, with some kind of Indian piece of silver and turquoise on a chain around his neck. His slacks were deep crimson and his loafers were brightly shined.

What he said was simple enough, and if he hadn't been lying, Dewey would have believed him. But you could look at him and see what he was. He thought he was above the law, above anybody's justice. He was here in the courtroom to oblige, not to be tried.

As his fingers raced along, Dewey remembered the old days in Bourbon Street. It had been an outskirt of hell. Women debased, enjoying their shame; men worse than animals, their very senses deranged by whiskey, their minds dissolved in lust and an appetite for disarray. He could barely remember a sequence of bawdy nights there, and the great overarching sense of freedom he had felt. Anything was possible. All was permitted. The deadly sins were a catalogue from which you could pick whatever you chose. Pederasty, violence, gambling, robbery, filthy pictures, whoredom—what was there that the mind of man might contemplate that could not be accomplished on Bourbon Street? So long as it was indecent, destructive of the soul? And then that hot August day.

Dewey shuddered as his fingers did their work. He wondered if his years in Shreveport had made up for his sojourn in that place. Who knows? He would wait and shudder until Judgement. What had he done but put the evil aside? Had he ever, even once, struck out against it? Was it enough, to be justified, to flee evil? Or must it be confronted, struggled with, vanquished? Was it sufficient to carry on that struggle within one's own soul—or must it be carried dauntlessly into the world?

Then Vallee began his questioning. What had happened that night? Had there been . . . sex?

Santidy was smiling as the questioning began, but his expression became progressively more serious as Vallee pressed on. At the mention of sex, Santidy hung his head like a chastened peacock. As if, on the instant, his flaunting manner faltered, and he suddenly shed years, became younger, more innocent. Dewey watched and could hardly believe.

Yes, Santidy whispered. Yes, there had been sex. God help him.

Vallee was silent for a long moment. As if ritual words had been spoken. Then, most quietly: — Tell us about it. We want to know, to understand.

He had gone often to Jumbo's after work. He was a stranger here, but the promise of good honest work had brought him east from California. He had worked in Texas,

then in northwest Louisiana. He would come down to
Shreveport to break the monotony, to see people enjoy
themselves. To find enjoyment of his own. A lot of oil men
came to Shreveport, to Jumbo's. It was a friendly place.
One could enjoy himself there in a decent manner: a few
beers, a few laughs with friends.

Yes, he knew Miranda. Everyone knew Miranda. Of all
the girls at Jumbo's, she was the loveliest, the most interest-
ing. She was very friendly, and she made him feel less lonely.
Bakersfield, California, is a long way from Shreveport. But
Miranda's smile made the distance less awful, less depressing.
Jumbo's was a real nice place, and Miranda was part of
the reason.

Dewey frowned. Only a little while ago, Vallee had been
talking about what a bad place it was, how a girl who
worked in such a place should know what men who fre-
quented it really wanted. Now Santidy was making it out
to be a home away from home. The jury will notice that,
Dewey thought. They'll have to notice that.

Vallee asked Santidy if he had offered Miranda a ride
home that night. Santidy smiled, looking a little confused.
He didn't understand. Vallee reminded him that Miranda
had made that claim. Santidy shook his head slowly.

— No, she must have forgot. It was the other way around.
She . . . asked me.

And he had been perhaps the least bit hesitant to give
her a ride. Yes, he liked her, but he had heard remarks—
nothing specific, more often a single word from one of the
boys, accompanied by a quick smile. Words and expressions
that might make one wonder.

Vallee paused, acting as if he were surprised to hear such
a thing. — What kind of words? Santidy shook his head.
He had sisters at home. He would never smear a young
woman's reputation. His people never tolerated such a thing.

Vallee glanced at the jury, as much as to say, see how

much all this unpleasant business pains this boy? — We've got to know, Alberto. You've got to tell us. You understand that, don't you?

Santidy nodded sadly, cleared his throat. They had said that Miranda was a punch, a tramp, that she went from man to man, that she was insatiable, and no one man—or two or three, for that matter—could satisfy her. Of course, Santidy had not believed that for a moment.

Caswell was on his feet, objecting, demanding that the testimony cease until he could lodge a continuing objection to this blatant hearsay. Vallee grinned, claiming that the testimony led toward framing defendant's state of mind at the time of the alleged incident, hence was admissible. Judge Lambert pursed his lips, ruled sustaining the objection. Vallee shrugged, smiled reassuringly at Santidy, and began again.

Dewey found himself sitting at the stenotype, fingers motionless. Testimony was over, final arguments closed, and he could hardly remember a word of it all. Judge Lambert was charging the jury, giving them the law upon which they were to judge the facts presented to them in testimony and by document. Dewey watched dully as the jurors listened, their faces revealing nothing. Finally the instructions were done, and the judge sent the jury to deliberate. The courtroom emptied slowly. Miranda's brother came up to assist her, casting a venomous look at Santidy and Vallee. Murray came up and sat at counsel's table near Dewey as Caswell wiped his face with a large pocket-handkerchief.

— That son of a bitch *is* gonna walk, Murray said. — He's not gonna serve a day or an hour. He's got it made.

Caswell nodded. — You got that right. Vallee's got the formula down, and old Santidy is a superstar. Why, that boy could bring Miranda's brother around if he had a little time.

— I believe that greaser could rape every woman in Caddo

Parish, one at a time, and still walk. He'd only have to spare twelve of 'em, Caswell said.

— How's that, Dewey asked.

— Why, he ought to leave enough to make up a jury to acquit him.

— Hell, Murray said angrily. — Maybe a couple he stuck it to would vote for him. You never know. Not nowadays. You can't know. How could you?

Caswell shrugged. — Youall want some coffee? We can walk down Milam Street to the Grille. They're not coming back for an hour or so. Take 'em that long to argue themselves out of following their old-time instincts.

Murray and Caswell and Dewey walked downstairs and outside. The air was cool and crystalline. Only a few cars moved down Texas Street, mostly in the direction of the bridge to Bossier City. Caswell and Murray moved ahead of him, and Dewey paused in the deep shadow beside the Confederate Memorial. It was large and graceful, a spire reaching up into the leaves of the ancient live oaks, pointed toward the cold and distant stars. At the four corners were granite busts of Lee, Jackson, Beauregard, and Allen. High above, looming under the canopy of oak leaves that circled like a garland, was the figure of an anonymous Confederate soldier. He stood, rifle between his broken shoes, staring north out of stone eyes, as if tonight, this very night, it all might begin again, and he was ready for it. Dewey stared upward, feeling for the first time in all his years in town, in the courthouse, that this place was a shrine. He could not say just what it meant, but there was something. Something ravished, taken by force, something lost and gone now. And these generals had fought and spent years of their lives to protect that something, to save it. That nameless soldier had died time and time again for its sake. Dewey felt himself blush with shame for some omission he couldn't

even bring to mind, much less name. He averted his eyes
from the monument, as if in darkness it still shown too
bright for him.

— Hey, Dewey, you comin, Murray called back to him.

— Yes, Dewey said, and walked on after them.

II

The jury filed in, and it was over in minutes. Not guilty.
One of the women on the jury was sobbing, but another had
something close to a smile on her lips as Santidy came forward to shake hands with them, thank them for their vindi-
cation. Dewey watched as if he were viewing a movie, as
if what he was seeing had little relation to reality at all, and
none whatever to him. He turned slowly, as Judge Lambert
discharged the jury, obviously displeased, but not enough
so to speak his mind as on occasion he did. Caswell sat
sweating, a smile not unlike that of the woman juror's on
his lips. Behind him, Dewey caught only a fleeting glimpse
of Miranda, her brother helping her on with her coat, and
speaking loudly words Dewey couldn't make out for the
commotion. But Miranda was paying no attention to her
brother. She was looking across to the defense counsel's
table, not at Santidy, but at Vallee, and her expression was
one of horror so profound, so all-encompassing that it
shocked Dewey, making him recall the face of a dead man
whose body he had once come across in an alley off Ursu-
lines Street in the French Quarter. While he was a beast.
That was how Miranda looked: as if she were about to die,
enthralled by the last and most brutal indignity we all must
surely suffer. As she turned away—no, was turned away by
her brother, who was still talking, something made Dewey
turn back toward the defense table where Vallee sat with-
drawn into a pool of silence, insulated from Santidy who
stood next to him laughing with some of his friends from

Oil City. On his face, Vallee wore an expression of cynical and analytical certainty almost as absolute and embracing as had been Miranda's mask of horror.

He's happy now, Dewey thought. He's just planning to do it again. He just waiting for the next one to come knocking on his door. He's a rapist, too. Just like Santidy.

— It's no use living in a country where this kind of shit can go on, Murray was saying. — I mean, it wasn't a sign of justice . . . Not a sign.

They were at Murrell's Grille on Kings Highway. Caswell was eating eggs and grits and sausage. He had stuffed his mouth with biscuit, and thus was forced to listen to Murray's tirade. Finally he finished chewing, shook his head.

— Goddamn it, Murray, what is all this justice crap? You been around the court as long as I've been lawyering. Why does this one stick in your craw. Hell, you and I seen a lot worse. Remember the Culpepper case?

Murray turned pale, put down his fork. For a moment, his expression was very still, very distant, as if he were having trouble keeping his food down.

— I don't remember no Culpepper case, Dewey said, trying to remember some case, some situation so monstrous that it would gag Murray.

— You wasn't up here yet, Caswell said, his eyes fixed on Murray. — This was way back before the war. I was in law school. Old man lived in Dixie Gardens—near Murray, matter of fact . . . Caswell laughed as Murray, still speechless, motion him to shut up.

Caswell grinned. — It was a tough case. Ask Murray about it some time . . .

No one said anything for a long time. They ate. Murray still shivering. Caswell finished his last biscuit, and Dewey sat thinking.

— He did do it, didn't he, Dewey asked at last.

— Huh, Caswell replied.

— Santidy. He did it to that girl, didn't he?

Caswell's eyebrows rose as he chewed. He swallowed and grinned. — What do you want, Dewey? You want me to give it to you in writing? I wouldn't have prosecuted the son of a bitch if it didn't look like he did. Beyond a reasonable doubt. But *did* he? I wasn't there. Maybe he asked nicely, and she changed her mind right in the middle . . . Maybe he forgot to ask . . .

Caswell picked up the check, took a few dollar bills out of the pocket of his vest.

— I really need to know, Dewey said quietly. — I do.

Caswell looked at him with amused weariness. — You've changed, Dewey. Hell, I remember when you used to do a hell of a job reporting and kept quiet. Maybe it's age. Maybe we all done our jobs and kept quiet too long.

Caswell stared out the window behind Dewey into the dusty empty street beyond.

— You know what, Dewey? I don't know whether that lousy California greaser done it or not. And I'll tell you something else. If I'd been there that night, if I'd been in the car watching, I still might not know. Things have their own way of happening, and sometimes you can't say who did what. Maybe it wasn't no crime at all. Maybe it was just . . . bad manners.

Caswell swung his bulk up out of the booth, and started toward the cash register. — I can't spend the night joshin with you boys. I got me an armed robbery over in Division G in the morning, and I flat *know* what happened there . . .

Caswell paid and left, and Dewey looked at Murray, who was still shook up a little. — He didn't have to mention Culpepper, Murray said. — I mean it's been a long day. He didn't have to bring that back . . .

Dewey stared at Murray. — What the hell was the Culpepper . . .

Murray shivered. — Forget it, he said, and rose from his

seat. — Just forget it. It was a long time ago, and you don't want to know.

They left then, climbed into Murray's car. Murray was shot, worn out, shaken. He didn't want to drive. Dewey barely knew how since he had never owned a car of his own. But he got behind the wheel and started out, driving stiffly, carefully down Kings Highway toward Murray's home, which he had never seen, never been invited to. When they reached the house, Murray asked him to spend the night on the back porch. There was a daybed there for friends who might stay over. Dewey thanked him, and they went into the kitchen for a nightcap.

Murray brought out an unopened bottle of Old Overholt and cracked the seal. It was harsh and rich, and Dewey felt as if he'd been in that kitchen every evening for years. Murray had control of himself now, and threw down two drinks for every one of Dewey's.

— I get drunk every night, Murray said, his tongue going loose, his eyes angry. — You didn't know that. Well, it's so. I come home from typing up them goddamned transcripts, and I get drunk. Ever since the war. Almost every night. I may have got to live in this shit-eating world, but it ain't nobody said I got to do it cold sober. No, I don't have to do that.

Murray got more excited as he drank the rye whiskey. He got up, opened a cupboard above the gas stove and brought out a Colt automatic and laid it on the oilcloth of the table.

— It's a .38 special on a .45 frame. Customized. Best automatic pistol in the world. Take a look. No, pull the clip and push back the receiver.

Dewey picked up the gun. It was lighter than it looked and felt smooth and reassuring in his hand. As if he had held it many times before.

Murray was mumbling now, to himself, drunk, nearly to

the point of collapse. — If I could just get that lousy, filthy
bastard in the sights of that . . .

— Santidy?

— Yeah. Him or . . . Culpepper . . .

— What did Culpepper . . . ?

— Forget it. If I could get that spic in my sights . . . Oh,
Lord . . . I never did get no Jap or German in my sights . . .
You know what I mean?

— I guess so.

Murray was close to passing out. — It ain't no justice left
in this . . . world. You know that?

Dewey finished his third drink. He had not put the
atuomatic down. — Yes, he said after a moment. — I guess
I do . . .

Murray shook his head, drunken tears flowing down his
cheeks. — It ain't no justice, I can see that now.

He staggered to his feet and picked up the bottle of rye
whiskey. — I'm going to bed. I can finish this in my bed.
You know something, Dewey? I throwed away a leg. It
wasn't no use. I never killed one of them sons of bitches,
but even if I had, it wasn't no use . . . wouldn't have helped
anything at all.

Murray vanished into a dark hallway, and Dewey could
hear him fall against something. Murray cursed, and then
there was silence. Dewey looked at the whiskey in his glass
for a long moment, remembering that Murray had been a
typist. He hadn't killed anybody. Then Dewey drank his
whiskey down.

He lay on the daybed with a pillow under his head. It
was deep night now, and he could see the stars through the
screen of the porch. Millions of them standing in the sky
unmoving. There were insects strumming against the screen,
and he could hear the naïve chatter of tree frogs just beyond
the porch. From the distant bayou, he heard the deeper,
more assured drone of bullfrogs.

Dewey lay quiet for a long time, thinking, trying to make his mind focus, but it was no use. There were only images passing across his mind like the motes that pass across the surface of the eye, which can never be seen clearly because they are part of the eye and move as the eye moves. He could not remember anything very clearly. It seemed as if the trial had been a long time ago, perhaps the day after he had come to himself in the French Quarter. Or the day he had arrived in Shreveport.

Dewey could not remember clearly when he had not been a reporter. Reporters were pledged to put down the truth in the cause of justice. That was hard to do in the midst of a trial, but he had always managed. And that had been enough. Other people had other things to do, but that was what a reporter did, and no one could expect any more.

It was then that he noticed he still had the pistol in his hand.

III

His knuckles were white, his fingers drained of blood, as he held onto the steering wheel crossing the Texas Avenue bridge into Bossier City. It was very late now, and there was little traffic, but the lights of Bossier City were still on. At the foot of the bridge on the left, he could see the Hurricane Lounge, a sign out front that said, WITH MAJOR AT THE PIANO. Down on the right, the Ming Tree, farther on, the K-9, and the Kickapoo Lounge and Motor Courts. Then the lights began to fall away, and the signs said U.S. Highway 80—the highway to Mississippi, to Monroe and Vicksburg. He drove another mile or two, until he saw the stark white plastered building that said TOWER LOUNGE AND MOTEL and on the right, smaller, lit not by neon piping, but by old-fashioned bulbs, JUMBO'S LOUNGE, Live Music Nitely.

Dewey pulled into the large parking lot and turned off

the key. He took off his glasses and wiped them. He was sweating, and they had fogged up. Now that he was here, he could not quite determine what he should do. No, that wasn't right. He knew what he should do, but he couldn't figure out exactly how to do it. He had never planned such a thing before, had never even imagined himself involved in such a thing. That was a bad handicap, because you couldn't practice this as you practiced shorthand or steno-type.

He could go inside, find him, and do it. Whether he was caught made no difference. But there was always the irreducible possibility that someone might stop him, deflect his aim. Then it would all be silly and useless, like the trial, like his life—and justice would lose again, be raped by his incompetence.

It would be easier to wait. Outside no one could stop him. Out here it would work. Then it occurred to him for the first time that Santidy might not be there, that already he might be with some other young woman, willing or not, in one of the greasy motor courts he had already driven past. Dewey had no idea what kind of car Santidy drove, and suddenly he felt his own determination draining away. It was silly. Murray was right. There is no justice any longer, and only its withered institutionalized wraith keeps things from flying apart.

Well, all right, Dewey thought. Maybe that's so. But we got to do our best. The Lord never asked a man for better than his best, did he?

He got out of Murray's Dodge and stood under the stark blue lights that rendered the parking lot almost as bright as day. He pushed his glasses close to his eyes and stared at the door of the place. Out of the corner of his eye, he saw on his right a sudden glitter, as if someone had turned on a light and quickly extinguished it again. He looked over there, and could see no more than a blur. I ought to check that out, he thought to himself. If I'm going to do this right, I ought to check out everything, hadn't I?

He walked behind Murray's car, and along the rank of cars parked on his right, squinting at each one in turn, inwardly embarrassed at the idea of playing at detective, a grown-soft old man who knew nothing of rough trades, but who had a thing that needed to be done, nonetheless.

He had gone perhaps twenty yards, past a dozen or so cars when he stopped. He frowned for a moment, forcing his eyes to focus on a long dull line of metal along the fender of an old Ford that was parked pointed directly at the door of Jumbo's. He squinted and stared until he could make out, behind the barrel of the rifle the low-lying silhouette of a man. He was on his knees, propping the rifle on the car fender. He looked tired, and the barrel of the rifle wavered, catching the parking lot lights, then losing them. Dewey watched the man, studied him. He was not a stranger. Dewey had seen him before, and even not able to identify him, somehow his presence inspired Dewey.

That means he's here, Dewey thought. — Somebody else wants him. That means he's got to be here.

Dewey stood behind the line of cars, silent, his eyes on the man with the rifle. It never crossed his mind that the man might be waiting for someone else, someone besides Santidy. That never occurred to him. No, the question was, should he speak to the man—or wait and see what happened.

It's important, Dewey thought. I really got to decide. Would it be just as good if some stranger done it? Or is it something I got to do myself? That's what I got to decide. What counts? That it gets done? Or that I do it?

It was then that for some reason he remembered the Confederate Memorial in the court square. Not so much the great men at the four corners, but most especially that single anonymous infantryman at the top of the column, that Confederate soldier without a name who stood, almost a hundred years later, still faithful in memory to his people and his duty. Then, remembering, Dewey began to move toward the rifleman, his own decision made. There was something that had to be done, and he had to do it.

But before he had taken more than half a dozen steps, before he could make himself known to that distant anonymous rifleman, the door of Jumbo's opened, and amidst a burst of laughter, five or six men came out. They were all drunk, having a good time. The first one out almost stumbled down the three steps. The others seemed almost like an escort for this first.

He steadied himself, then came down the steps smiling, his arms around his fellows. Dewey squinted across at the rifleman, trying to be sure. The man at the foot of the steps was surely Santidy. Dewey couldn't make out his words, but he could hear the boasting, self-important tone. He was the center of attention, and the others listened to him, hardly trying to put in their own remarks. Of course. Why not? He was the hero tonight, wasn't he?

Dewey stared down the length of the car toward the knot of men. As he did so, he realized that the man kneeling in front of him had hunched forward, his right elbow up, and was leveling his rifle at the group. Oh, Christ, Dewey thought, he's going to do it.

— No, Dewey heard himself whisper harshly. — No, Mister. Don't do it.

The rifleman turned, his face pale, distant, as Dewey came abreast of him and moved just as quickly past him.

— Wait, the rifleman said, his expression one of astonishment and recognition. — Ain't you the . . . ?

Then Dewey recognized him. It was the brother. The girl's brother. Miranda's brother.

— Wait, he called after Dewey. — You got no business . . .

His voice fell away as Dewey came out from between

the cars and moved more quickly toward the men standing, talking, laughing at the foot of the steps of Jumbo's place.

Dewey pushed his glasses back again with his left hand as he came near them. They paid him no mind, and he could see Santidy up close now. It was easy to recognize him. He wore white slacks and a red shirt with a white vest over it. His hips moved as he swapped words with his friends. He made an expansive gesture with his hands, as if in some way he encompassed the world with his actions. It was a good night, a wonderful night. Maybe the best night of his life. Wasn't that what he was thinking?

Dewey pulled the .38 out of his belt as he came close to the men, and one of them saw him coming. The man was short and had sandy hair that looked as if he used grease on it. He called out shrilly, but Dewey paid him no mind. As he closed with them, now only yards away, he saw that all their faces seemed a strange, sickly blue as if they were not human at all but some species of degenerate creature that spent its life in moist caverns where the light of day never reached. It was the hue of the lights above the parking area, of course, but Dewey did not make that connection then. He was in motion.

—Christ, the sandy-haired one said, and Dewey remembered later how preposterous the name of Our Lord sounded in the mouth of a beast.

— Hey, what is it, another called out when he suddenly saw Dewey. As if he expected an answer, an explanation.

What Dewey saw was the tight slacks that Santidy wore. He had no consciousness of aiming and firing. All he thought about was Santidy's skin-tight pants.

The first explosion surprised him as if he had somehow not expected the gun to make such a noise. He paused for the smallest part of a second, shaken by the sound and its immediate echo off the front of the building. Those around Santidy melted away as if they had been no more than mist, projections of his own ego, or as if this strange show were not happening in the physical universe, but on some theological stage, and they had received their cue to exit. But the surprise, the instant of hesitation did not really even slow Dewey down. Now he was facing Santidy who stood alone. They were alone in the sterile blue of the dusty parking lot. Time had stopped, Dewey remembered thinking. It was not happening in the world. Not this.

— Aw, Christ, Santidy moaned, staring down at the crotch of his white slacks, ruined by Dewey's first shot.
— Aw, Jesus, Santidy sobbed, staring at the bleeding ruin between his legs.

Dewey stepped still closer then, until he could have reached out and touched Santidy with his hand. But he didn't touch him. He raised the pistol just as Santidy looked up, his eyes hollow and distant and almost objective, as if somehow, even in his hour of triumph, he had been aware in his blood that judgment was on the way, that retribution was no less sure than physics, and that between his acquittal and that doom there might just be time enough for a few drinks, a few laughs.

— Aw Christ, Santidy moaned again . . . Mister, he crooned, — Mister, for Christ's sake . . .

The sound of the second shot did not surprise Dewey. What was amazing was how Santidy seemed suddenly to rise from the asphalt of the parking lot and hurtle upward into the door of the roadhouse.

— Mister, Santidy whispered, the front of his white vest suddenly as red as his shirt, the shirt itself glistening with a hue it had not had before. — Mister. Then he slid down against the door and sat quite still, his eyes locked on Dewey's.

— All right, Dewey heard himself say. — All right.

He turned and moved back then toward Murray's car. He looked from side to side, the pistol up and ready, but the lot was empty. He knew that Santidy's friends were somewhere, behind the cars, across the highway calling the police. But they were not coming for him. He had expected they would be armed, but even that might not matter. As he neared the old Dodge, he realized that he had never expected to get this far. But he had, and he was still alive.

He had gotten the car door open when a figure materialized beside him so suddenly that he almost fired before he recognized the brother, Miranda's brother.

— Don't try to stop me, Dewey said. — I ain't done. I know you're an officer of the law, but it had to be done. It should of been done by the court . . . That's where it should of been done . . .

The brother moved back as Dewey climbed into the car and started it up. He began to back out, the motor roaring because of Dewey's unfamiliarity with motorcars and his rising nervousness. It was hard to control his hands and feet. As he fought the car into first gear, he could hear over the motor's roar the voice of the brother.

— Mister, thank God for you, you hear . . . ? Mister, thank God . . .

Dewey straightened out the car and pointed it toward the highway, taking his foot off the gas for only a moment.

— You're a good man, Mister . . .

Dewey looked at the harried young man still holding his unfired rifle, his face covered with tears either of tension or thanksgiving, and then awkwardly aimed the car out into the highway as he pushed hard on the gas.

IV

After he had gone a mile or two, he slowed down. He had said something to the brother that he himself hadn't understood. What was it? He frowned and wished he had drunk more of Murray's Old Overholt. There was something else that needed doing. But perhaps it could not be done tonight. He had done a good thing. His fingers eased around the steering wheel, and of a sudden he began to notice and enjoy the cool breeze blowing in the driver's window of the car. As he passed between the lights of Bossier City, he thought that perhaps he should have bought a car. For drives on the weekends. He could have gone to Texas to see the sights in Marshall or Gladewater. He felt relieved, fresh, buoyant. He had not felt so good in a very long time. Since he had fled New Orleans so long ago? If not, since when?

When he reached the Shreveport side of the bridge, he slowed down still more. He began to consider what would come next. There was a building, two or three stories tall, at the corner of Milam and Spring streets. But it was so late. Perhaps he should go back home, or to Murray's, and see to the end of his business tomorrow. He realized that despite the freshness, he was very tired. Couldn't it be done to-morrow, the rest of it?

No. If nobody had recognized him except maybe the brother, still people had seen the car. They must have. It wouldn't work tomorrow. No matter how tired he was, this was the time. They had been tired at Mine Run and Me-chanicsville. For no reason, an old song popped into his mind. Now is the hour. That's right.

He twisted the wheel and turned left, almost coasting down Milam Street. When the light changed, he took an-other left. He inched down Milam block by block, until he reached Spring Street. Then he pulled to the left curb and parked. For the first time, he realized that he was a little drunk. Not dog-drunk, but drunk nonetheless. Outside, the single street light seemed to expand and contract as he watched it. That was how he knew he was drunk. Then there was a sinking feeling in the pit of his stomach as he noticed that the street light was the same awful stark blue as those at Jumbo's parking lot.

He shouldn't have drunk so much, he thought. This is important. It's the only important thing you ever did in your whole life, and you had to get drunk to do it. And you'd like some more. You'd like one more drink before you finish up. If you can finish up, which is doubtful at this hour.

Dewey leaned forward, his head on the steering wheel. He felt sick, drained. He called to mind the scene in the parking lot, Santidy staring down at his ruined groin. It had been like a dance, with Dewey leading. Santidy for the first time in his life playing the unwilling maiden, moving away, declining, praying, falling backward, bereft of his weapon, knowing at last what it meant to be raped. Terminally.

Dewey's head rose, and he laughed, the sound more shocking than the reports of the pistol at Jumbo's. Not from the remembrance, or even from the drink. No, it was that he suddenly recalled what Father Ruiz used to say back home at the parochial school when some wayward boy required discipline: Knowledge maketh a bloody entrance. — Sure enough, Dewey heard himself say. — That's so, Father. Like opening a door and seeing something awful.

The remembrance and the laughter sobered him a little. He got out of the car and walked up to the front of the office building. The building was brick, painted white. The door was locked, and Dewey stared at it stupidly for a moment. Maybe Vallee wasn't there in his offices. In fact, it was silly to think he would be. After a long trial, after a big victory. But no. He *knew* Vallee was inside. He *knew* it, had known it ever since the moment in front of the Confederate Memorial when he decided what he had to do. Vallee would be in there.

Dewey looked around, then wrapped the .38 in his handkerchief and hit the glass of the door. There was no alarm, and a section of the glass fell away, crashed with little sound on the inside. He reached through and opened the door quietly. As he stepped in, he squinted at the shabby building directory barely illuminated by the blue light from the street. Then he moved quietly down the dark hallway. As he did so, he could see no light from any of the doors on either side of the passage. If Vallee were in there, wouldn't there be some light from under his door? But the number had been a large one. One-thirty-three. Maybe it was so far in the back that the light was invisible from here.

As he walked on, he almost tripped and fell as he reached a flight of steps that went up to a landing, then down again. At the top of the landing off to the left were the stairs to the second floor. He looked down toward the back of the first floor. There was light coming from under a door. Not much light. Hardly enough to be coming from a desk lamp. Maybe Vallee had come here alone, celebrated with a few drinks, and fallen asleep; it would be necessary to awaken him. Maybe he was just taking care of last details regarding a case he thought he'd won, but which Dewey had reversed only a little while ago.

Dewey reached the door, listened. It seemed he could hear something inside, something hardly louder than heavy breathing, but he could not be sure. He turned the door-knob very slowly. To his surprise, it yielded, and the door swung inward silently.

For a moment Dewey hesitated, then moved into an unlit, cramped reception office. No wonder the light had been faint. It was coming from under another inside door marked Private. The sound Dewey had heard was louder now, and it sounded not so much like breathing as moaning. For a moment it crossed Dewey's mind that perhaps someone had been here before him. Miranda's brother, the young policeman? Could he have come here before he went to Jumbo's? Or maybe some outraged spectator in the court? God knows there was cause enough. What if it was so? What if Vallee was already lying in there dying? What if

her brother had done for him? Should Dewey just turn
and walk away? Was that sufficient? He thought not. Let
every man put his own mark upon wickedness. Perhaps,
before morning, there would be a veritable parade of just
men who would make this pilgrimage. In fact, Dewey
thought, I better get done what needs doing before somebody else shows up. He reached for the knob of the door
marked Private realizing with a strange feeling that he had
never in his life gone through a door so marked without
permission—much less to murder the inhabitant. He heard
the moaning more animated than before. The sound puzzled
him. Then he heard the sirens. They seemed to come from
Texas Street down near the bridge. That would be the
Bossier City Police. By now, the confusion surrounding
Santidy would have been worked through. They would
have tracked the car to the bridge. They would find it soon
with the help of the Shreveport Police. Only minutes to
go. He turned the knob and pushed the door open, still
quietly, the sound no louder than the moans within, which
had turned now to snufflings, gruntings, choked syllables
almost like human words. As the door opened, the sounds
broke off with a sharp intake of breath.

Vallee sat in a large chair facing Dewey, his eyes almost
closed, his face contorted as if in excruciating pain.

— Ahhhh, he sighed.

And Dewey saw in the weak light of a desk lamp turned
away the head of a woman between Vallee's legs. When
he realized what he was seeing, he staggered back a step in
astonishment. The woman was kneeling in front of Vallee,
and he was pulling her into his groin, masses of dark silken
hair in his fingers.

As Dewey stepped back, Vallee must have heard him
because his eyes opened and he stared, with an absurd smile
on his lips, into the gloom where Dewey stood. The smile
remained plastered on his swarthy face even after the first

bullet had knocked him backward almost out of the chair when it plowed into his chest. Dewey fired again, lower, to erase what he was seeing, but not fast enough, because even as he fired, fired again and again until the hammer snapped futilely, he could still see the face of the woman as she turned out of passion into death. He could see her face even after the bullets had obliterated it, and he knew that he would go on seeing it until his last breath.

When he closed the door, he was still controlled. It had not fixed itself on him yet. He looked at his hands. There was a trembling, but not much. Only when he heard, from beyond the door that now said Private again, a heavy breathing, a snuffling and moaning certainly sounding of death, did he begin to run. He tripped up the stairs and down the far side, almost fell as he ran down the hall toward the blue light, and out into the sudden chill silence of Milam Street. He kept running until he reached Market Street. Then, winded, he slowed down. Walking a little farther, he stepped into the doorway among the display windows of Selber Brothers and stood silent, listening.

Sure enough, there were sirens, and down behind him, near the Pioneer Bank, toward the river, he could see police cars. But that was all right now. He crossed the street against a red signal that stopped nothing in the empty street.

Under the oaks in the courthouse square, it seemed cooler still as Dewey walked down toward Texas Street, cutting across the corner of the square, already seeing looming before him the shadowed mass of the Confederate Memorial. Dewey paused before it. Down to the right, at the edge of his vision, he could see the stark shining cross atop the First Methodist Church. To his left, the lights on the bridge. The sirens were still at that end of town. They might have found the car by now. They might have found more than that.

Lee, Allen, Beauregard, Jackson, Miranda. Dewey's hands

reloaded the exhausted clip of the .38 as if somehow they
were independent of his mind. Jackson. Miranda. He could
not protect her. No one could. No one could be protected.
Not Lee or Allen could protect anyone. It was. A lost cause.
He thought, they don't build monuments to them any
more. Because they don't want to be protected. They hate
the ones that fight against the very nature within us.
Santidy. Vallee. And someone.

Then Dewey felt the tears running down his cheeks and
the enormous weight of the gun in his hand. He was immediately very tired. Tired as he had been that hot afternoon
in the French Quarter in New Orleans long ago, before
he came to himself. There was just no sense in being this
tired. Nobody ought to put up with it. His eyes tracked up
the monument until, in a light now gray, not blue, he could
make out the distant face of that other anonymous soldier
there. Now the secret was revealed. He had escaped. In the
heat of battle, he had found the stone.

The sirens began again, and under their shrieking, Dewey
could hear the waking murmur of the courthouse pigeons.
It was almost dawn, and an empty Broadmoor trolley passed
down Texas Street on its first trip out to the edge of town,
and Dewey drew a deep breath of relief as he realized he
had only one thing left to do. And then he would be free.